Ciel

SOPHIE LABELLE
TRANSLATED BY DAVID HOMEL

Second Story Press

Library and Archives Canada Cataloguing in Publication

Title: Ciel / Sophie Labelle ; translated by David Homel.
Other titles: Ciel. Comment survivre aux deux prochaines minutes.
  English
Names: Labelle, Sophie, 1988- author. | Homel, David, translator.
Description: Translation of: Ciel. Comment survivre aux deux
  prochaines minutes.
Identifiers: Canadiana (print) 20200212389 | Canadiana (ebook)
  20200212850 | ISBN 9781772601367(softcover) | ISBN
  9781772601374 (EPUB)
Classification: LCC PS8623.A23235 C5413 2020 | DDC jC843/.6—dc23

Cover illustration by Sophie Labelle

All emojis designed by OpenMoji—the open-source emoji and icon project.
License: CC BY-SA 4.0

Printed and bound in Canada

*Second Story Press gratefully acknowledges the support of the Ontario Arts Council
and the Canada Council for the Arts for our publishing program. We acknowledge
the financial support of the Government of Canada through the Canada Book Fund.*

Published by
Second Story Press
20 Maud Street, Suite 401
Toronto, Ontario, Canada
M5V 2M5
www.secondstorypress.ca

For Mémère

1

Don't Call Me "Young Man"

You might not believe me if I tell you, but I have a special power. It's not my fault; it's just the way my body works. Like a kind of magic. And I don't believe in magic, so that gives you an idea…but here it is—every morning, no matter what time I set my alarm clock, my eyes open exactly two minutes before it rings. I swear, it's true. If I set the alarm for 5:45, I will beat it by two minutes. If it's for 6:30, my eyes pop open at 6:28, if it's supposed to ring at 7:07…you get the picture. I can't do anything about it. Even if I try to close my eyes again, it won't work. Something in my brain keeps me from going back to sleep, even though I love sleeping. Instead, all I can do is stare at my alarm clock until two minutes go by. As soon as it rings, quick as a cat, I hit the Snooze button before my father, my brother, or my dog has the chance to wake up. Quick as a ninja!

There it goes. Five thirty-five. *Beep! Beep! Beep!*

I've never mentioned my special power to anyone, not even my best girlfriend, Stephie, because I'm afraid people won't believe me, or they'll think I'm so weird they'll send me to take all kinds of tests to see whether I'm a mutant or something.

I turn on my light, slip out of bed, and put on pajama bottoms and a T-shirt, the first clothes I can find. No need for fancy rags for my job.

For the last few months, I've been delivering the newspaper. But even before my job, I would wake up very early for no other reason than to see the sunrise and listen to the songs of the birds. I live near Rosemont Boulevard in Montreal, on a street so quiet I can hear everything that's happening at night while everyone is sleeping. My house is right next to the Botanical Gardens, and this last summer I went there often to read or play on my Nintendo Switch after I was through with my paper route. Now that it's September, the sun rises later and it's still dark when I'm delivering the paper, but at least the birds are singing. And if I'm lucky, I'll see a fox.

Once I get dressed, I unplug my phone from the charger to see whether Eiríkur answered my last email.

He lives in Iceland, and with the time difference, it's day there. But he doesn't go on the Internet very often, so even if I answer his messages as soon as he sends them, it takes him a few days before he lets me know he's still alive. That bothers me sometimes. After all, we're supposed to be a couple.

The home screen on my phone is a picture of the two of us in Maisonneuve Park just before he left. He seems a lot older than twelve, the opposite of me. His broad shoulders, which once comforted me, make me look smaller than I am, and in the sun, his hair is so blond it's almost white. In the photo, my hair is still short. I don't think the style looked good on me, but it did make my green eyes greener.

He went back to his home town, Reykjavík, two months ago. (Don't ask me how to pronounce the name of the place, I tried once and Eiríkur laughed at me.) He spent two years, maybe a little more, in Montreal, with his father and mother. He has a sister studying in England, and I met her when she came for Christmas. She was a lot of fun. He and I were in the same class in grades five and six. His father is a video game designer, and he was hired by a Montreal company to work on a big project. Unfortunately, his contract ran out last May. Since his mother develops Internet sites, and she works for herself, she could go back to Iceland to live,

3

and they did. I thought that was selfish of them since they knew Eiríkur and I were going out together, and now all we can do is send emails and call each other on Skype once in a while. I talked to my father, and he promised we would go visit him next summer, but that's ten months away. We'll have time to break up and make up five times before then.

I check the messages on my phone. No reply. Eiríkur is as lazy as they get. I'm not really mad at him because he's always been that way. When people say I'm lost in space, I tell them they should meet my boyfriend! At the beginning of grade six, when we started going out together, Eiríkur admitted he'd been trying to tell me he loved me for six months, but he kept putting it off. I had to ask him to be my boyfriend. He's so shy, and I love him that way. But he should have made an effort to send a message. He knows today's my first day of high school, and I'm stressed out to the max.

It's a new school, which is part of the trouble. It's much bigger, with at least five times more students than at Joe-Rose, where I went last year. All the kids from Joe-Rose will be there, and ones from other grade schools from the neighborhood too. It's intimidating, being around so many people I don't know. I don't like having to explain who I am to everyone.

You see, I'm transgender, which means I identify

with another gender (whether it's boy, girl, non-binary, or any other) than the one the doctors gave me at birth when they looked at my genitals (which are nobody's business, by the way!).

People like me have always existed, all around the world. There is nothing new about us. It's not abnormal; it's just the way part of humanity is made. In most societies, it's the custom to attribute a gender to newborn babies, without waiting to ask their opinion. Depending on whether they're designated a girl or a boy, their rooms are painted a certain color, and they're given certain kinds of toys to play with. Afterward, if people turned out to be wrong, and the children end up being a different gender than the one that was assigned, why would they have to justify themselves and explain the mistake to the doctors and their parents? If you ask me, trans children shouldn't have to explain anything, and adults should say they're sorry instead of bothering them.

In my case, I'm not exactly a girl, and not really a boy. I am somewhere outside these two. And that has nothing to do with what I like to do or the clothes I wear. It's the way I feel in the world and how I want people to understand me. Usually, it bothers me less if they think I'm a girl and call me *she* than if they think I'm a boy. But what feels right is *they*. *They* can mean any gender. It's been used for people like me for centuries. Usually, the first thing people wonder about when they hear that I'm trans is what's in my pants. That's not very polite. I know that might happen, very soon, when I walk into the classroom. Do you think there are people anywhere in the world who like talking about their private parts in front of a bunch of strangers? Count me out!

When someone asks, I have to explain that when I came out of my mother's stomach, the doctor exclaimed, "It's a boy!" But he didn't take the trouble to ask me what I thought, which isn't very nice, especially since I've never really been a boy. My parents made the same mistake as the doctor, and gave me a typical boy's name, Alessandro. That's the name the teachers are going to call me today, even though I don't like it very much. That's what they called me in grade school, and it didn't suit me. With a name like Alessandro, no wonder people think I'm a boy. I'd rather be Alessandra.

Most of the time I ask people to call me Ciel. That's the name I've been using on the Internet the last few years. I like it because it doesn't sound masculine or feminine.

My boyfriend, Eiríkur, isn't transgender. But he's bisexual, which means he can be interested in people of any gender, including mine, apparently. Everything is much more complicated than you can imagine. Sometimes I wonder whether Eiríkur fell in love with me because he's bisexual. But he doesn't worry about those details. He tells me my gender makes no difference to him, and that he loves me, Ciel, for everything I am, completely.

♥ ♥ ♥

One of my favorite things is feeling the warm wind on my face when I'm on my bike. Especially early in the morning, when the air is still wet with dew. I have time to think, I'm alone with the birds, and sometimes the fox, as I deliver papers from house to house.

Of course, it's not the most exciting job in the world. It's very repetitive, and the same things keep happening over and over. Sometimes a dog, inside a house or an apartment, will wake up and bark as I'm going up the steps to the mailbox. Or I'll come across a raccoon serving himself from the garbage cans as if they're a buffet, but that's about it.

I'm trying to save enough money to buy a real camera to make better YouTube videos. I have my own channel called *Ciel Is Bored*. I've put a few videos online, but they're not very good since I made them with my phone. I talk about my dog, how the day went, how I feel, stuff like that. It's fun, and it passes the time. I have twenty-one subscribers, and some of them I DON'T EVEN KNOW! My goal is to have thirty by the end of the year. I might have to make some friends at high school.

The last stop on my route is the wealthy-looking house with the porch. Doctor Mahelona lives there. I like him because he gives me the biggest tips. They don't have to, but most people leave me a little envelope in their mailbox with a few dollars inside. Every Thursday, in the doctor's mailbox, there is a little plastic case with a sticker on it, and my birth name written there: Alessandro Sousa. Inside, a five, ten, or twenty-dollar bill. The earlier I deliver the paper, the higher the amount. The doctor goes to work before everyone else, and he likes to read the paper over breakfast.

I met up with him once, very early in the morning, as he was going off to work at Maisonneuve-Rosemont Hospital. He was happy to see me. And he explained his system for the tips. Since I want to buy the video camera I've had my eye on as fast as possible, I've been trying to go for the twenty-dollar amount.

But there's a problem, it's a kind of trap. To get to his mailbox, I have to go up an asphalt walk with bushes on both sides, then climb the steps to the porch. That's where the doctor keeps his big recycling box and his garbage cans. And since they are emptied only once a week, on Fridays, a lot of the time raccoons are rummaging around inside. They might be the cutest animals in the world, with their little paws and their fat stomachs, but I can't help being afraid when I hear them knocking over the cans and squealing.

I leave my bike on the sidewalk and creep up to the porch. Carefully, I lift the metal top of the mailbox. There's the transparent plastic case—with a twenty-dollar bill inside! I smile, slip the money into my pocket, and put the case back where it was.

Then, accidentally, I drop the metal cover of the mailbox. *Clang!* That's when one of the garbage cans tips over and a raccoon goes somersaulting through the air. He tries to escape across the porch, then he sees me, switches direction, and bangs his head against the wall of the house.

I drop the newspaper and take off.

It's light outside by the time I get home. I park my bike in the backyard and lock it to the back stairway that leads up to our apartment. I go inside without making a sound. I tiptoe across the kitchen and down the hall that leads into the living room. My little brother Virgil and my father are still sleeping, so I can go onto the computer and check to see if anyone new has viewed my videos since last night.

I should have known. My foot lands squarely on a Lego spaceship my brother left in the hall, and I yelp in pain as the pieces crunch together, then go flying across the wooden floor. Right away, Borki, our dog, jumps off Virgil's bed to come and see what is going on. He doesn't bark (good dog!), but I know that an excited dog scrambling over my brother will be enough to wake him up. Well, it's not my fault.

I turn on the computer and see that I have no new comments on my YouTube channel. By then, Virgil is standing in the kitchen, pouring a bowl of cereal.

"You want some toast?" I ask him.

He shakes his head. You can't expect much out of him in the morning. But I'm not complaining. It's better than someone talking nonstop. I like Virgil just fine, but he's a real chatterbox when he gets going. And he's only nine years old. I hope it's not one of those conditions that worsens with age.

I make myself a peanut butter and jelly sandwich and swallow it down without even chewing. Borki nibbles on our feet under the table, tickling my brother and making him laugh with his mouthful of cereal. My father comes into the kitchen, yawning. He teaches chemistry at a college, and with his schedule, he can stay in bed later. Usually, he gets up to make our lunches if he hasn't done it the night before, or just to tell us to have a good day, then he goes back to sleep once we leave. He smiles, runs his hand through Virgil's hair, then opens the fridge to take out our lunchboxes that are ready to go.

My father's name is Gabriel Lucas Sousa. He's from Brazil and he came to Montreal when he was a student. At first, he planned on staying for six months to study, then he met my mother, who's from here, and they fell in love. After his studies were over, he returned to Brazil, then spent the next summer here, then left again, but came back for good. I was born, he got a job at the college, then Virgil was born, then we adopted Borki, and with all that, he couldn't really go back to Brazil, even if the rest of his family (except our Uncle Guilherme) still lives there. And even if my mother died five years ago.

I get along with my father really well. I can tell him anything, and he'll understand. And if he doesn't, instead of getting mad, he'll think about it, and dig deeper. That's what he did when I told him I wasn't a boy or a girl, just after my mother died. He smiled and said, "All right." Then he held me in his arms, which was a real relief. A few days later, I saw a pile of books in his room about trans people. My father's pretty cool.

I hear the sound of a spring popping—*Boing!*—from my room, which is my alert for text messages and emails. I put my plate in the sink and go see who it is (maybe Eiríkur finally got around to answering my message).

Ready for the torture chamber, my dear?

It's Stephie, my best friend. She's transgender like me. We've known each other since kindergarten, back when, like me, people thought she was a boy. But we didn't really become good friends until grade four. Stephie transitioned at nine, and unlike me, she's 100 percent a girl.

You're kidding! I'm still in my pajamas

Come as you are, you'll knock 'em dead!

Dream on

Did I wake you up?

Of course not

Too bad 😉

Stephie and I have this game. We score points when we wake each other up. She has more points than I do. It's not fair, because she doesn't sleep much, and when she does, she's impossible to wake up.

See you at the locker?

You bet!

I started harassing Stephie last June to share a locker together. Last year, at our old school, I was twinned with Eiríkur, but that's impossible now. I wanted to be sure I'd be with her because I don't have a lot of friends, and I didn't want to be stuck with just anybody. Who knows who it could have been?

At first Stephie thought she'd share with Frank, her boyfriend, but I guess she took pity on me. Anyway, it's not like Frank doesn't have loads of friends he can share with. He's super popular, and at our old school, he was one of the best soccer players.

I get undressed in a hurry and throw open my closet doors. I want to wear something discreet for my first day at school. Not very easy: all my clothes are pretty flashy. Last year, the other kids in my class knew me well enough not to bother me about that, and I felt comfortable wearing whatever I wanted. But I'll have to start all over again. I'm not going to pull out the spangles on the first day! My father bought a lot of things in the "Young Man's" section, just in case, but admit it, they're as dull as dust. Some of them are prettier, like this salmon-colored sweater I wore a lot last year, but the way the sleeves drop from the shoulders, it just shouts out "CALL ME YOUNG MAN."

That's the last thing I want to happen on my first day of high school.

I decide to wear the white shirt with the lace on the front that I got for my birthday, the beige jacket that's too big for me, and a pair of black leggings. With that outfit, I will achieve both my goals: I won't be too visible, and people won't mistake me for a boy too much.

2

Trouble at Simonne Monet-Chartrand

I took a quick trip through Monet-Chartrand High School the day I registered. I remember more or less what part of the building my classes are in, but the hallways are so endless they make me dizzy. There are three levels: first, the ground floor, where the atrium is—the big open space where people hang out before classes—and the lockers, stretched out along the yellow corridors that smell a little like mold. Then there's the second floor, with the cafeteria, and the third floor with the little auditorium that is also used for school meetings and assemblies. The classrooms occupy the second and third floors. The student entrance is on the ground floor, and leads directly into the hallway where the first-year kids have their lockers. That's where I'll be.

The locker that I share with Stephie isn't in too bad

shape. I brought along the little stuffed crocodile my father gave me last week, and stick her tail into one of the slits in the door.

Stephie comes skipping up.

"How's it going, cutie pie?"

"Don't call me that!"

"Okay, don't lose your cool. What's with the green stuffy?"

"Georgette the crocodile. I figured she could be our locker mascot."

"I like her already!"

She starts transferring the contents of her backpack onto one of the two top shelves. No one would ever guess we're friends by looking at us. There's me, with my long, messy chestnut hair, my mixed-up clothes, and my dazed and confused look. Then there's Stephie, with her smooth, dark hair, her soft smile, and her shiny little ballerina shoes. She's so pretty, if you ask me.

I remember how happy my father was when Stephie and I became friends. It was in October, we were in grade four. After my mother died, two years before, I didn't talk to anyone. During recess, I would get harassed by grade five guys who called me "fag" and "fairy." One day, Stephie heard them. She got so angry she started yelling at them, and they ran for cover. She really scared them! Back then, she used to wear pink dresses and animal barrettes in her hair (she'd kill me if she knew I was telling you that!). She looked like the perfect little girl.

After that, we started hanging out together at school, then she invited me to her house. We dressed up and she painted my nails. I felt a lot better, not just because she was nice to me, but she made me feel I didn't have to dress like a boy. My father let me wear what I wanted to at home, but I was afraid people would make fun of me at school. Stephie had so much self-confidence that being with her helped me slowly feel more comfortable at school. When he found out I was friends with Stephie, my father called her mother, and wanted to meet her. They still talk a lot. Apparently, having trans kids makes people come together.

Once her backpack is empty, Stephie leans against the locker next to ours.

"All ready for today?"

"More or less. But I'm sorry I didn't have my name changed on the teachers' lists, the way you did. I'm going to get called by a boy's name for the rest of the year."

"You've got ten minutes before the bell to make up your mind. You could go see your teachers and explain. My mother met mine last week, to make sure they would act the right way with their trans students. She asked them to be discreet about me."

Stephie's mother, Alice, is very involved in everything that has to do with trans people. She teaches sociolinguistics at the university. That's like social studies, but less boring. She's on TV all the time, and journalists consult her if they are writing something about trans issues. Though Alice isn't trans herself. It's funny how they trust non-trans more than trans people when it comes to our experiences.

Actually, Stephie could have gone and talked to the teachers herself. So could I have, if I had decided to. I could have done a few tap dance steps for them while I was at it, why not?

"I hope your mother told the teachers to give us As and no homework."

Stephie laughs. "Right! Otherwise they would be guilty of being transphobic."

I can always make her laugh. That's my role in our relationship, and I like it. Besides, that way people think I'm bursting with self-confidence, even if the opposite is true. Stephie leans over and whispers to me.

"You won't forget, right? Not a word about me being trans. We won't even bring up the subject. I'd like to be something other than that 'trans girl' this year."

"But there are plenty of people from our old school here."

"I know that. But I want to have the chance to start

all over with the new kids. You can bet I'm going to do that!"

She told me all about it the last time we talked on the phone. We call each other a lot. She wants to be less visible at school and make more cisgender friends. That's the word for people who aren't trans. I understand her. When the kids at school always see you as different, you end up feeling exhausted. And you know that the way you're different is going to influence how people act toward you. But I don't know if I could do what she wants to. I'd get stressed out if I thought someone might "discover" that I'm trans once they're friends with me. I'd be sad to see how they would change once they "discovered" who I am.

Now that I know about her plan, I wonder if that means I'll have to make sure we're not seen together too often. It's harder for me to hide the fact that I'm trans, since I'm much less a girl than she is. If they see that we're always together, people could make the connection and guess that she's trans too. I would feel bad if I ended up ruining her plans without wanting to.

I spot Frank, her boyfriend, sneaking up behind her. He motions me not to say anything so he can take her by surprise. Too late: my eyes give me away, and she turns around. Frustrated, Frank gives her a last-chance hug, and she laughs at him.

"Why were you sneaking around like that?"

Stephie stands on her tiptoes to throw her arms around her boyfriend and kiss him on the cheek. I'm always amazed to see that he's a head taller than she is, after all those years of her being taller. How long have they been going out together, a year and a half? More like an eternity! The strangest thing is, before they started seeing each other, Frank was really nasty to her. In grade four, he would bug her and make jokes about her. If you ask me, that was his awkward way of getting closer because, strange again, after they did a team project together, they started being friends. I wasn't surprised when Frank asked her to go out with him, a year later. At first, she wasn't so sure, since she had feelings for a girl whose name I forget—Stephie is bisexual too, like Eiríkur—but I think she was so impatient to be with someone that she would have said "Yes" to anyone. In the meantime, Frank proved he can be a good guy. He and I don't have much in common, but we get along well enough. He's nice to me and warm. He doesn't really have a choice. I'm his girlfriend's best friend, and that's sacred.

He and Stephie finally remember I'm there, and get unstuck. Frank combs his short black hair with his fingers, a little embarrassed.

"You all right, Ciel?"

"Not bad. You?"

"I'll get by."

We met at Stephie's a few times during the summer, so this is not the most moving reunion in the world. Stephie takes one of her notebooks and slips it under her arm.

"Okay, time for us to go. Good luck with your first class! See you at noon here?"

"Yes," I tell her, with the bravest face I can manage as I watch them move off toward the stairway. My throat tightens as they go. Eiríkur always used to walk me to my classes last year. We would hold hands, discreetly, to keep people from bugging us. I miss him so much. And I don't think I know anyone in my math class. I'm off to a bad start.

I head for my classroom, thinking about what Stephie said. It's true, I could just tell my teacher I'd like her to use a different name from the one on her list. Then I walk in and see she's not even there. Unhappy, I move quickly past the other students, not meeting their eyes, and choose a table by the windows.

Three minutes before the bell sounds. Finally, the teacher, Mrs. Campeau, walks in. She looks pretty cool. Young, with short hair. I'm sure she would understand if I asked her to change my name. Do what Stephie did.

Hide the fact that I'm trans. But go up and speak to her in front of everybody? Too intimidating.

Two minutes left. I steal a glance around. I must not be the only one who's stressed out. Maybe there are other trans people in the class. People trying their best to disappear, like me.

One more minute. Some people come running in. A girl I don't know sits down at my table. She smiles. I smile back. The teacher gets up from her chair. I start to perspire.

The bell rings.

♥ ♥ ♥

"So, did you survive?"

As she promised, Stephie is waiting for me at our locker at noon.

"More or less. Aren't you with Frank?"

"He wants to eat with Viktor and his gang. What do you mean, more or less?"

"English was okay. But my math class…. The teacher is nice enough, but when she read out our names, she was so surprised when I raised my hand after she called mine that she repeated it, just to be sure. Then the girl sitting next to me looked and said, loud enough for everyone to hear, 'Are you a guy?' I pretended I didn't understand. But during the whole class, I knew she was analyzing my face, as if that could answer her question. I felt like a rat in a laboratory."

"No! Poor thing!"

"Don't worry, it wasn't so bad. With a little luck, the next time we have math, she'll go sit somewhere else, and I'll have the table to myself."

"I hope so! My morning was pretty dull. I had English first period, and the teacher put me right to sleep. But in biology, I was with Felicia and Annabelle. You remember them?"

"Kind of."

"We were in the same class for two years in a row."

"Really?"

"Felicia has braces and an Afro. Annabelle is tall, with glasses."

"Oh, of course!"

"She doesn't wear glasses now, she switched to contacts."

I went along with Stephie because I was embarrassed, but the truth is, I have no idea whom she's talking about. I have a lot of trouble remembering names and faces, and more likely than not, those two girls never spoke to me. A lot of times, people recognize me in the street, but I don't know where I met them. I must be spending too much time in a parallel universe.

"They asked me if I wanted to eat lunch with them. I said 'maybe.' You want to?"

"Sure, if you do."

"I made them promise not to tell anyone I'm trans. You might laugh, but at first Annabelle just stared at me. I had to explain what that meant. She looked at me, completely confused, then she said, 'Oh, I remember! You looked like a boy at the beginning of grade school. I thought it was just your style, you know, the short hair and everything. I never made the connection.' Meanwhile, Felicia squinted at me and didn't say anything."

"Hashtag OopsYouShouldn'tHaveSaidAnything."

We go up to the cafeteria on the second floor. Stephie spots the table where Annabelle and Felicia are sitting with some other people. They look vaguely familiar. Both of them smile when they see me.

The one with the Afro says, "Ciel! I'm happy you're eating with us."

Really? They even remember the name I chose. The tall one gives me a serious look.

"I was wondering if you were ignoring me in math. When you walked into the room, I called to you because I wanted us to sit together, but you headed straight for the window."

"Sorry, I didn't hear you."

"That's for sure! You looked completely lost in your thoughts."

It's more embarrassing than I thought. Sometimes I don't know which way is up. How come all of a sudden, these girls are acting like they're my best friends, when we never really talked to each other? Did someone cast a spell on them, so they think I'm super cool? Or are they so terrified to be in high school that they've lowered their friendship standards?

I'm happy to be part of a group, though it is a little strange. I'm not used to the company.

Stephie gives me an encouraging smile from her side of the table.

3

The Big Sibling

"Don't you think it's weird? That's the first time I've ever talked to them, and they act like we spent our whole grade school playing *Fortnite* together."

After lunch, Stephie and I leave the cafeteria, waving to Annabelle and Felicia.

"You're worrying for nothing. I'm sure they just want to see some familiar faces. Eating with us is their way of staying in contact with our old school."

"What if it's a plot, and they're spying on us so they can expose us to everyone?"

Stephie bursts out laughing. "Where do you come up with that stuff? You should let people be your friends sometimes. Not everyone is trying to get you."

We stop at our locker, where Georgette the crocodile

is patiently waiting. Stephie is in my French class, which is good, because it's the one I have most often.

The first bell rings. All around, people start moving, making a racket—the correct response to audible stimuli—like a pack of robots. Stephie and I grab our stuff and head for French. We have five minutes before the second bell.

The classroom is on the third floor. You have to take the hallway where we first-year students have our lockers, then cross the atrium in the middle of the school. From there, the main staircase leads up to the second and third floors. There's only one problem. The atrium is an intimidating place. From what I can see, between classes, dozens of students, most of them from the higher grades, sit on the benches and talk and laugh at the top of their lungs. Some of them even have beards! Worse, they stare at you as if you don't exist, looking right through you, as you make your way toward the stairs. Good thing Stephie's with me. Every time I have to walk past that spot, I want to disappear into a crack in the floor. That's how I feel when people look at me.

We climb the stairs, and I whisper to Stephie, "I wouldn't mind going to a school where everyone is trans."

"There wouldn't be many students there."

"Maybe not, but at least I wouldn't always be afraid

that people are making fun of me. And you wouldn't have to hide that you're trans."

"It's not that I want to hide it, I just don't want it to influence the way people treat me. If one person finds out, everyone will call me 'he' for the rest of my life."

"See? That wouldn't happen if we were at a trans school. You'd have something in common with everybody else. I was thinking of doing a video on the subject for my YouTube channel."

"You'd let the fact that you're trans define where you can go? That sure puts some limits on you."

"If I feel more comfortable that way, then why not? You know, since I left my house this morning, I haven't gone to the bathroom, because I don't want to go to the boys' or the girls'. I'm too afraid of the potential drama."

Stephie stares at me in disbelief. "You mean you've been at school six hours and you haven't peed?"

I pull on my jacket lapels, snapping my imaginary suspenders with pride.

"At least six hours."

"Why don't you go to the infirmary, like back at our old school? I'm sure there's a quiet place there."

"I don't know where it is."

Stephie sighs. Am I letting her down? She knows very well I'm not comfortable in places that are for boys only, or girls only.

"Listen, this is what we're going to do. The second bell rings in two minutes. The bathrooms will be empty, no one there but us. That's the best time to go."

"Are you sure? We'll be late to class."

"We'll tell the teacher we got lost."

On the third floor, we head toward the girls' bathroom, right next to the stairs. Two or three students are drying their hands in a hurry, then rushing to their classroom without looking at us.

The second bell rings.

Stephie pretends to check her mascara in the mirror as she keeps an eye on the door. I slip into a stall.

My heart starts beating faster. I hate walking into a class late, especially the first day, but the feeling of letting go, after spending hours holding it in, is really worth it. I flush the toilet, exit the stall, wash my hands quickly, then we sprint down the corridor that, unfortunately, feels like it's a mile long. Everything is going wrong!

When we reach the door, Stephie peers in through the glass.

"The teacher is taking attendance."

"Should we go in?"

"I suppose."

I look at Stephie, unsure. She looks back. Which of us will open the door?

I put my hand on the doorknob and turn it slowly to make as little noise as possible. I let Stephie go in first, and follow her to a table at the front of the class, where there are two free chairs. No one wants to sit in the first row, especially not on the first day.

Our French teacher, Madame Walter, is tall, and about my father's age. She looks up from her class list and considers us in silence as we settle onto our chairs. When she speaks, her voice is kind.

"I won't mark you as absent this time, but don't make a habit of it."

Stephie must be worried. Her reputation as a perfect student is in danger.

"Sorry," she answers, "we were in the bathroom."

Madame Walter lifts her eyebrows, then visits her list again.

"Let's see, who did I mark as absent… Stephanie Bondu, I suppose?" she says to my friend.

"Yes."

"Then you must be Liam Johnson?"

I feel all the blood in my body rush to my face and I turn fire-engine red. There is not a drop left for my fingers and toes, that start trembling as if it were the middle of winter. Some kids behind me, maybe from my old school, start to giggle.

"No."

"What's your last name?"

"Sousa."

"I see. I hadn't gotten to the S's yet. Alessandro Sousa?"

For a split second, that seems like an eternity, a wave of contradictory thoughts washes over me. Then I answer in a voice so strong it surprises me.

"No. It's Alessandra, with an A. There was a mistake at registration."

Madame Walter takes off her glasses and looks at me, surprised. Then, before going back to her attendance sheet, she adds, "I thought it was strange, a girl and a boy going to the bathroom together. With your voice, if you had short hair, I would think you were a boy."

♥ ♥ ♥

After Madame Walter said that terrible thing, I heard a few bursts of laughter, and looked down to hide my shame. Stephie acted as if nothing had happened. I suppose she was relieved that the teacher didn't make her stay after school, but she must have been embarrassed at how Madame Walter said she thought I was a boy in front of the whole class. Sometimes I think I'm sabotaging her efforts to not be noticed. During the class, a little voice in my head kept telling me I should stop being her friend, to keep from ruining her life.

When the bell rang, I said good-bye as fast as I could and went to my ethics and world views class. I was still in no mood to talk about what happened. Not right away, in any case. My feelings were still too hurt.

Back home, Virgil is crashed out on the sofa, his feet in the air, watching cartoons, the way he always does. He looks away from the screen long enough to say "Hello." I'm pretty lucky with my little brother. The only time he gets mad is when he wants to follow me and he can't, like when I sleep over at Stephie's, or go to the LGBT+ Youth Center (twelve years and older only).

Ever since he was little, he has been calling me his "sibling" instead of brother or sister. At the house, he likes to wear my dresses, and sometimes he asks me to style his hair. But only at the house, never at school. He loves to try all kinds of things, even if he continues to identify as a boy.

I push away his stinky feet and make room for myself on the sofa. We watch TV for a few minutes. Then I break the silence.

"I want to make a new video for my YouTube channel."

"Cool! Can I be your cameraman again?"

"The last time I let you film, it looked like there was an earthquake, the picture was jumping around so much!"

"The wind was blowing. It wasn't my fault."

"Yeah, sure. I thought I'd go back to the park, like last time. It's a good place."

"Right now?"

"Right now. What happened at school is still fresh in my memory."

Virgil isn't happy about having to turn off the TV before the show is over, but I promise to buy him licorice after the shoot, and that's enough to get him leaping off the sofa and putting on his shoes. I send a text to my father to tell him we are at the park, so he won't think we've been kidnapped. Then I go into the bathroom and make an attempt to fix my hair, and apply some styling cream, which always looks good in a video.

I lock the door on the way out as Virgil rushes down the metal stairway to the street. I catch up to him a minute later.

"What happened today at school?"

"Actually, things went okay, except I didn't see a single bathroom that wasn't either for boys or girls. I had to wait till everyone was in class before I could take a pee while Stephie guarded the door, and we were both late.

Then my French teacher told me that if it weren't for my long hair, she would have thought I was a boy."

"She's mean!"

"I don't think so. She didn't even realize that might hurt my feelings."

"Then why do you want to make a video?"

"Because I'm tired of everyone acting as if people like me don't exist."

The sky is cloudy, but I read on the Internet that it's better that way if you want to film. Too much sun gets in the camera's eye, or something like that. We spend ten minutes looking for the best spot in Maisonneuve Park. It's one of the biggest in Montreal, but you can't get lost because the Olympic Stadium tower is your landmark. The Stadium is south of the Park, and we live north. To find my way home, I just walk in the opposite direction from the tower.

Virgil is starting to get impatient. "How about there?"

"No. Look at that bush, it's ugly."

"What about over there?"

"With that big street in the background?"

"Then up on the hill!"

"There are no trees or anything."

I'm a bit of a perfectionist when it comes to my art (and when it comes to torturing my little brother). But it's important. Since he admires me, I need to maintain my status as a legend, and that means taking my YouTube pastime more seriously than it really is. That way, other people will take it seriously too. I read that on the Internet as well.

Virgil points to a clearing surrounded by lilacs, red maples, and apple trees. To make him feel good, I congratulate him, because the place is perfect. Well, "perfect" is a big word. Let's just say it's adequate. To be perfect, it would need chairs, a little table with a water glass, and a fox in the background.

I check my phone to make sure my hair isn't too much of a mess, then I hand it to Virgil, who sits in front of me. He counts down, "Three...two...one.... Action!" But we both know I'm going to spend the first few minutes saying silly things and making faces, to warm up. Maybe more than a few minutes today, since I want to talk about a subject that's important to me. Most of the time I talk about easy things, like the trouble our dog gets into. Not that Borki isn't important, but today, it's different. Finally, I'm ready. I dive in.

"Hi, this is Ciel, from *Ciel Is Bored*. Today was my

first day of high school, and…uh, I think it went pretty well."

I take a deep breath. My lungs feel completely empty. Then I launch in for real.

"But, actually, no, it was a complete mess. I discovered that my new school doesn't have any washrooms I can use, since they are all separated into boys and girls. I had to hold it in the whole day. But then I couldn't stand it, and I waited until there wasn't anyone in one of the girls' bathrooms, and I went there. Because of that, my girlfriend who was with me and I were late for class, and that was the excuse the teacher needed to make comments about me. First she thought I was a boy, then she said that if I'd had shorter hair, she wouldn't have thought I was a girl, not with my voice."

I take a moment to catch my breath. I think I went too far with my tirade, because my cheeks are hot and the muscles of my face are tense. That doesn't happen when I talk about Borki. Sitting in front of me, Virgil encourages me to continue.

"I'm really sick of comments like that. And sick of not having washrooms adapted for us. Why do all girls have to be alike, and all boys the same? We're not copies of the same model."

I stop and think. I am going much farther than I planned to.

Then I look into the camera for my conclusion.

"Well, it's easier to ignore those things, and force everyone to fit into two different boxes, one for girls, the other for boys, and too bad for the rest. This is Ciel, from *Ciel Is Bored.*"

4

Practical Advice in
Case of a Zombie Attack

I open my eyes at 5:33, two minutes before the alarm is set to go off. In the dark, I stare at the red dots that flash between the hour and the minutes. I feel more tired than usual, but my special power to wake up before the alarm has not deserted me. Though it was a lot easier during the summer when I didn't have to go to school after my paper route.

I turn off the alarm clock, then push aside the blankets to look for my phone. It's Tuesday. My last email to Eiríkur is a week old, and he hasn't answered. I know that's normal, coming from him, but it's too long for me. I even wrote him a message on WhatsApp last Friday, giving him the link to my latest video. I worked fast to edit it and take out the worst parts, and post it as quickly as possible, so it would be up-to-date.

Sometimes it takes me weeks to upload a video, because I'm lazy. Which is why I understand it when Eiríkur takes his time answering me.

On Friday, I gathered up my courage and went to see my teachers before class to ask them to change my name on their class lists. I will be Alessandra in French, social studies, science and technology, art, and gym, and Alessandro in English, math, and ethics and world views. That's a little strange, but what can you do? I think it went pretty well. My gym and science teachers were in a hurry when I went to see them, and they just said, "All right, that's fine." The art teacher was a little confused and didn't really understand what I was trying to tell him. If you ask me, he's always lost. He must have thought I was a cisgender girl. On the other hand, he has never taken attendance, and doesn't seem to want to know the students' names. No wonder he couldn't understand me coming and telling him I wanted to be called by a different name.

I wasn't very busy this last weekend. I didn't do much besides read mangas, ride my bike with my father and my brother, and listen to music. I felt nostalgic for the days when Eiríkur lived just two blocks away. When I wasn't with Stephie, I'd go to his place and we'd hide out in his room and play video games and read graphic novels all day. Once, for total darkness, we stuck big pieces of cardboard over his window. It was the perfect atmosphere for his zombie game. I've never been a big video game fan, but I was happy to share one with him.

I know I'm going to be spending more weekends by myself, now that Stephie wants to make new friends. We never talked about what happened during French class. And I didn't dare call her on Friday evening to ask if she wanted to come to my house. I knew she was going to visit her grandmother in Sherbrooke for the Labor Day weekend. She put photos from her hike on Mount Orford on Snapchat.

I put down my phone and sigh. I spend too much time online! I throw on my clothes and go pour myself a glass of guava juice before heading out on my paper route.

Every morning around four o'clock, a truck from the newspaper office drives past and someone drops off the pile of papers I'm supposed to deliver. What they do is more like throwing than dropping, since they pitch the bale onto my porch. Sometimes the racket wakes me up.

That's part of my morning ritual, opening the front door and having a stretch as the sun begins to come up. I bring in the bale of papers, cut the white plastic band that holds them together, and stuff the copies into my bag. Usually I have time to glance at the headlines in case there's something interesting. This morning, when I see the word *transgender* written in big letters, I drop my bag and start reading:

A young Montreal transgender person wins gold at the Canadian junior swimming championship

Liam Johnson, a 12-year-old athlete, has struck gold: the boy from the Rosemont district won a gold medal at the Canadian Junior Swimming Championship that took place this year in Whitehorse, Yukon. His participation made waves a few months back, as he was the first transgender person to sign up, which forced the competition's organizing committee to review its selection process. The committee's decision to include Liam Johnson attracted international attention, since it meant that transgender youth required no medical certificate to compete in the gender category they identified with.

This is a triumph for young Liam, who was born with a girl's body, but who has not undergone a sex-change operation or hormone treatments. When questioned about it, he said he intended to begin taking testosterone soon in order to masculinize his body, a procedure that is unfair to other competitors, according to some analysts. (See SOCIETY section, page S-1)

I feel like tearing up the paper and burning the whole pile. Are you kidding me? The boy wins a gold medal in a national championship, and all the journalists want to talk about are his genitals? That makes me mad! And the way the article talks about the new rules for the competition, as if the committee's decision not to discriminate against trans people was an act of great generosity. It's really frustrating. And can someone tell me why the piece is in the "Society" section instead of in "Sports?"

At least the photo that goes with the story is good. The champion is in his racing trunks, ready to hit the water. A lock of his curly brown hair peeks out from under his cap, next to his right ear. His eyes are alert, as if he were concentrating on nothing but winning. I take a picture of the article with my phone to show it to Stephie later on.

Then I put my bag over my shoulder and go out the back door into the yard, where my bike is. The article is still running through my head. Liam Johnson? Funny, I've heard that name before….

♥ ♥ ♥

"Our locker is turning into a regular palace!"

"I was thinking of installing a solid gold toilet, right here on the shelf."

Stephie laughs as she looks at her reflection in the little mirror I hung on the inside of the door. The frame is as green as Georgette the crocodile, and the words *Too Cute!* are written above it. I found it at the drugstore yesterday and convinced my father that our locker absolutely needed it.

As Stephie makes faces in the mirror, I ask her, "How was your grandmother's?"

"Not bad. We went hiking on Mount Orford."

"I saw the pictures."

"You haven't seen this one!"

Stephie takes her phone from her pocket and shows me a photo of a plate with a slab of gray, floppy meat on it and a salad.

"Ick, what's that?"

"My grandmother got it into her head that I adore calf's liver, even though I hate it. She wanted to spoil me, so she cooked some for Sunday dinner."

"Sounds delicious! Is it just me, or is she always trying to get you to eat something inedible?"

"She does that all the time. The last visit, she served me blood sausage for breakfast. Blood sausage! Can you imagine? She swore I had told her, once upon a time, that I liked it. Not very likely! I forced myself to eat most of it. Anyway, enough of that. Here's some other photos of Orford. That's the summit."

I point to a baby-faced boy in one of the pictures.

"Who's that?"

Stephie clutches the phone to her heart, then raises her eyes in ecstasy.

"Sebastian Fontaine. He was hiking with his parents, and we exchanged phone numbers!"

I put on a fake exasperated look. "You're collecting them now? You want me to tell Frank? When's the wedding?"

"Never would be too soon!" She laughs. "All he could talk about was his mountain bike. But he's so handsome. Look at his legs!"

She blows up the photo of that part of his anatomy and pushes the phone in my face. I deflect her arm.

"I get it, he has legs, I saw them."

Actually, I think it's funny. Even if Stephie has been going out with Frank forever, and their love will probably survive the downfall of civilization, she can't help falling for any guy who comes along. She's a hopeless romantic.

She gives me an elbow to the ribs.

"What did you do this weekend?"

"Not too much…. I edited my new video so I could

put it on YouTube. I went biking with my father and my brother. Virgil had friends sleeping over, so I bugged them a while."

"Sounds like fun!"

"Then I harassed Eiríkur on WhatsApp so he'd answer my email."

"He hasn't answered yet? Forget about him!"

"He's busy."

"By 'busy,' you mean he has too many video games to play?"

"Give him a chance, the new *Zelda* just came out."

"I don't think it's fair that a game would come before you," Stephie says.

"It's always been that way. It's not that games come before me, but he falls into them and can't get out."

I don't like this conversation very much. I know that Stephie's intentions are good, but she's too hard on my boyfriend. I decide to change the subject.

"What about your guy? Isn't he supposed to come see you this morning? Or did he fall in love with someone with legs too?"

"He texted me. He's a little late, so he's going right to class. He had a soccer game last night."

"Did his team win?"

"Since when do you care?"

"I just want to know if he earned the right to be late!"

Stephie slaps me on the shoulder and I laugh. I like teasing her about Frank. The two of them are so much in love, they seem to be the only two people on Earth in their sweet little cocoon. I wish I could have gotten that close to Eiríkur before he left.

The first bell rings. We hurry and close up our locker, then move toward our class. We have French first period, and since we sit together, we go in together.

Stephie talks away as we climb the stairs.

"Since you want to know, Frank's team won, thanks to Frank, who scored two goals."

"Some legs he must have!" I tease her. "Did I tell you he's in science with me?"

"You sent me a dozen photos of his back during class."

"It's not my fault. He was sitting right in front of me with his friend with the brown hair."

"Viktor?"

"If that's his name. You know what? I took your advice."

I tell her how I had my name changed on the attendance sheets for my Friday classes. Stephie doesn't understand.

"But that means you won't have the same name for all your classes. The students who have more than one class with you won't get it."

"If it's like last year, they'll ignore me."

"You don't understand. Lots of people care about you, whether you believe it or not."

I laugh. I'll believe her the day I spend fewer weekends alone at the house, being bored.

We turn down the hallway that leads to our French class. Just seeing the door has me feeling stressed out, the way I was last Thursday, when Madame Walter got my gender mixed up, right in front of everybody. I'm glad Stephie is in the class. Otherwise, I wouldn't have the strength to go back into the room.

We go to the same table as last time, in the front of the class. Stephie waves at a couple of girls in the back. Before the bell rings, I glance at my phone and see I have a YouTube message: a new comment on the video I posted Friday. Stephie tries to read it.

"What does it say?"

"Someone I don't know, 'Friesandcheeseandgravy,' who said, 'Very good video! Important to discuss these things. Hope the rest of the year goes better.'"

"That's sweet!"

"I hope whoever it is will subscribe to my channel."

"Hey, you have almost a hundred views for your video."

I smile proudly, in spite of myself. Stephie always encourages my projects, like my YouTube channel, but even when she doesn't try, she ends up being better than I am. Last year, she created her own channel to post a video without words, just filmed cardboard signs on which she'd written a story denouncing transphobia at school. The video was viewed more than fifty thousand times, it was talked about on TV (her mother Alice was interviewed), and she ended up with a few thousand subscribers, without having to put anything else online. More than once, she wanted to cancel her channel, and every time I convinced her not to. I'm a little jealous, and I think she feels bad about getting so much attention when she doesn't really want it.

The bell rings. I put away my phone, and everyone stops talking. Madame Walter puts on her glasses and takes out her attendance sheet. She makes a joke about hoping she can remember everyone's name. When she calls Stephie's name, my friend squirms next to me as if she were just dying to tell the teacher not to call her "Stephanie." Everyone calls her "Stephie." It must be strange for her when someone uses her full name. But she answers "Present" without saying anything.

The teacher goes on with the attendance. "Liam Johnson? You weren't here Thursday?"

I look up when I hear the name. A little shiver comes over me. I turn around slowly. I can't believe it. It's the cute swimming champion who was on page one of the paper this morning! There's no mistaking him. He has the same bright eyes, the same dark, curly hair. I slip my phone out of my bag and show Stephie the photo I took of the paper. Very carefully, I point at the screen, and discreetly nod in Liam's direction.

"No, I wasn't," he tells the teacher. "I have a letter from the office explaining why."

He opens his notebook, and Madame Walter reads the note. Stephie takes my phone, reads the headline, stares at the boy, and mouths "OMG."

"Alessandra?"

"Present!" I answer, quickly lifting my head.

Madame Walter gives me the evil eye.

"Put away your telephone, please. I have a feeling you're going to be a problem for me this year."

I blush and slip my phone back into my bag. I'm amazed. What a discovery! Liam Johnson showed his letter giving him permission to be absent without even mentioning he missed school to win a gold medal at the Canadian Junior Swimming Championship. He doesn't seem proud, or anything. He looks straight ahead, too relaxed to even smile, but with a sweet look on his face. He's in complete control. I'm impressed. He must be too cool to be my friend.

♥ ♥ ♥

I go into the cafeteria and sit down next to Stephie, who is already at the table where we ate last Thursday and Friday. Those two girls from our old school are there, Felicia and Annabelle. By now I can tell them apart, since Annabelle and I sat together in math, right before lunch. Two other girls are at the table too. I don't think I've seen them before.

Stephie does the introductions. "Zoe, Samira, this is Ciel, my best friend."

"I know you. We have English together," Samira says.

"Oh, yeah, that's true," I tell her, embarrassed.

I must have blushed, because in English, the teacher calls me "Alessandro," and I don't correct him. Luckily, Stephie introduced me by the name I chose, so it's less awkward.

It's strange to eat with people like Zoe and Samira, who don't know that Stephie is trans. If they suspect anything about me, they don't let on. I always think I have to watch every word I say. I really want to ask Stephie to read the whole article about Liam Johnson (she usually thinks that clichés about trans people in the media are funny). But we promised not to bring up the subject at school. Talking about Liam, I wonder which table is his. I scan the cafeteria in search of the gray fleece he was wearing this morning. It's not easy.

There are a lot of people, and Liam is not exactly huge. The junior-level gold medalist in swimming is nowhere to be seen.

"But he's not that bad, really. What do you think, Ciel?"

"What?"

That would be Samira talking to me, and the whole table is staring. Seeing that my mind was elsewhere, Samira tries again.

"The English teacher. What do you think of him?"

"I don't know. He's tall."

"You don't think he's laying it on too thick?"

"Too thick?"

"You know, he sits on his desk, he's always telling jokes."

"I think he's funny."

"He's trying too hard, if you ask me. Like he wants us to think he's so cool."

Mr. Lessard, the English teacher, is all right with me. I laughed a lot in his class last Thursday. But when I think about it, I might have been the only one laughing. Sometimes, when I'm having fun, I forget the people around me. That's what my father says.

I don't want to doubt Mr. Lessard's good intentions, so I shrug my shoulders.

"I don't know, maybe you're right."

I avoid further discussion by digging into the meal my father made for me. I know it's a little childish, I'm in first year of high school, but my father is still making my lunch. He makes Virgil's too, and I think he really likes doing it, so I don't say anything. He always sticks a little Post-it inside, with a message saying, "Have a good day, sweetie!" or "Finish your lunch so you'll have energy in case of a zombie attack." I think that's cute.

As I bite into my sandwich, I look at my phone. What? Twenty-seven notifications on YouTube? I almost choke on my lunch. My most recent video was shared a hundred times since this morning, I have fifteen new subscribers, and more than twenty comments.

I can't believe it. I click on the video to see the number of views. Five hundred and sixty-two.

5

The Bitter Heart of Mr. Lessard

Tuesday evening, after school, I hurried back to read the comments about my video. Most of them were positive, and I added a lot of new subscribers to my channel, which is really cool. And some people liked my hair, and thought I had a pretty smile.

But I also got a large number of negative messages that were painful to read. Things like, "You're ugly" and "There are only two genders, didn't you ever study biology?" It was a strange and very unpleasant feeling to think that so many people I've never met hate me. When I showed my father the comments, he told me to look on the bright side. If they were insulting me, then they must think I'm important. Otherwise, they wouldn't pay attention.

Some people didn't agree with my opinions. They

didn't think teachers should have to make accommodations for trans students, and that schools shouldn't do that either. I don't think that's very fair, coming from people who will never have to experience the stress about which washroom to use. But at least they didn't insult me, and I didn't delete their messages.

When I showed some of the comments to my brother, he was terrified.

"They have no right to say stuff like that! I hope you'll go to the police."

I shrugged my shoulders. "The police won't do anything. It happens all the time. People are anonymous on the Internet. They do whatever they want. The only way to stop it is not to put more videos online, and take down that one, and get off YouTube."

"Are you going to do that?"

What was my answer? I strolled away, doing the cakewalk, a maneuver I learned in my tap dance class last year. And I hummed a victory song to celebrate the success of my channel.

I open the locker door with a sigh. I'm glad the week is finally over. It was pretty intense. Stephie rests her chin on my shoulder as I store my books on my shelf.

"You okay, Ciel? You look worried. You haven't said a word all day."

I turn my head slowly and look deep into her eyes.

"I hear voices."

Stephie retreats a step. Now she looks worried— very worried.

I smile.

"I'm just kidding you."

She hits me in the stomach with the notebook she's holding.

"Very funny!"

"It's because of what's happening with my YouTube video. I try not to think about it, and most of the time I succeed. But last night I couldn't sleep. I had all kinds of nightmares."

"Nightmares? My poor darling!"

"I shouldn't have put that video online. It's too much to handle. I just want it to be over."

Stephie squeezes my arm.

"That's the price of success." I know she wants to comfort me. "When I put up my video with the cardboard signs last year, I got the same reaction. With social media, it's hard to avoid. My mother deleted the nastiest comments so I wouldn't be upset."

Maybe she's right, but I still feel down.

She gives me a hug.

"Don't worry, Ciel, things will work out. Let's go have lunch."

We go to the cafeteria, to our official table, even if the school year is only a week old. The other girls are there and look happy to see us. In my mind, I go over their names. Annabelle, the tallest one. Felicia, with the Afro and the braces. Zoe, who has short hair. And the girl in my English class. Samira. Right.

I'm proud I could remember everyone's name, but I'm still not used to all these people wanting to sit with us. Stephie must attract them—she's like a magnet. She has this way of looking at people when they're talking, so that they feel interesting. I wish I was like her: sympathetic, relaxed, always smiling. If I wasn't her friend, I'm not sure those girls would even speak to me. For example, right now, there are five other people at our table, and not one of them is talking to me. Maybe it's my fault. I'm nervous and can't join the conversation. This is harder than being on my own. I feel like Stephie is dragging me down the hallways like a ball and chain.

"Hey, you'll never guess what Frank asked me yesterday!" she bursts out, interrupting my thoughts.

"Is Frank your boyfriend?" Zoe asks, interested.

"Yeah. He's sitting over there. See him? In the khaki sweater."

"Not bad," Zoe smiles. "His friends aren't bad either."

"Why don't they come and eat with us?" Felicia asks, wrinkling her forehead. "We could use some boys here!"

"His best friend Viktor thinks he's too cool for us," Stephie says ironically. "They've been in the same gang since grade five."

"What did Frank ask you?" Zoe wants to know.

I don't really listen to Stephie's answer. I start thinking about our gang last year instead. It was small, just me, Stephie, and Eiríkur, and sometimes Raquel, who was a friend of Eiríkur's, and hasn't spoken to us since he left, because after all, she's in a special music program now. Things were easier back then. I knew what to expect. I knew the school and everyone in it. But now everything is so new, and too complicated for me. I can hardly keep up.

I glance from table to table, hoping to spot Liam, and find out who he's eating lunch with. But he is nowhere in sight. He can't possibly have a table in the washroom!

Once I eat what's in my lunchbox and read the little message my father wrote ("I can't guarantee this lunch isn't haunted. Better eat all of it so the ghosts won't have anywhere to hide"), I listen to the other girls chatting away. A few minutes later, I gather up my things and stand up without waiting for Stephie.

"I'm going to my next class early," I tell them. "I have some questions for the teacher."

"What class?" Annabelle asks.

"Science and technology."

"Oh, no!" Zoe exclaims, full of sympathy. "Our teacher already gave us a test, and we have a whole chapter to read by Monday. Too cruel!"

I attempt a smile, then ask Samira shyly, "See you in English?"

"Right, see you soon."

Stephie waves, and gives me a questioning look.

Actually, I lied. I don't have any questions for my science and technology teacher, but I'm going to the classroom ahead of time anyway. I'm relieved to get away from those girls. I just don't feel comfortable with them.

Near the big door that leads into the atrium, there is a bulletin board with all kinds of notices and announcements. My eyes are drawn to a poster with the rainbow and the trans flag. I'd recognize the second one anywhere, with its pastel blue, pink, and white lines. I stop and read.

GENDER AND SEXUALITY ALLIANCE

First meeting of the Gender and Sexuality Alliance at Monet-Chartrand High School

Tuesday, September 12, join us in Room C-116 at 12:15 for some socializing and to plan the coming year's activities.

EVERYONE WELCOME!

We respect every person's sexual orientation and gender. Come as you are!

PIZZA WILL BE SERVED!

I take a picture of the poster. I'm intrigued. I've never been to a school where there was an LGBT club. Instead of eating lunch with people I don't know, I might as well be with students I have something in common with. Not to mention the free pizza, which is pretty hard to resist!

♥ ♥ ♥

At the end of science, as I'm putting my scarf back on, Frank walks up to my table.

"Hey, Ciel, how are you doing?"

He hardly ever talks to me when Stephie isn't around, except when we cross paths at school. At the beginning of the period, when he came in, he said hello, which is the most you can expect. I like Frank well enough, but it's strange to talk to him alone. We really don't know each other.

I decide to lay it on thick.

"The earth is burning up and the only thing humanity can think of is building more pipelines. Besides that, things are okay. What about you?"

"I'm all right. Except for the pipelines, of course. I saw your last video about bathrooms and your French teacher. Pretty good!"

I can't help blushing. "Oh, thanks."

I forgot that Frank had subscribed to my YouTube channel last month. That was nice of him. His compliment is encouraging, and I decide to open up to him.

"I've never had so many negative comments about a video. They haven't stopped since the beginning of the week."

"Really? That's a drag."

We fall into an embarrassed silence. I'm standing at my table, my notebook and pencil case under my arm and my scarf around my neck. He seems to want to tell me something. He scratches his head, then looks at me.

"I realize I don't have your number in my contacts, so I can text you. Can I have it?"

"Uh, sure, of course."

He opens his school calendar onto this week. No bright colors, no stickers, no nothing. Just notes written in pencil, impossible to read, with finger smudges everywhere. And the school year has just begun. I take a pen out of my case and write my phone number in the "To Do" section.

Frank smiles. "Great, thanks!"

He closes his calendar and hurries off to join Viktor, who is waiting for him by the door. A pretty strange encounter, if you ask me.

The rest of the day went by fast. In English, my last class, I sat with Samira, though we hardly talked to each other at all. She spent the period drawing in my notebook while Mr. Lessard, the teacher, tried to teach us irregular past participles. I don't know anyone else in the class except for Jeremy and Caleb, from my old school, and they hate me. They can't help themselves, they have to laugh at everyone who isn't exactly like they are. Sitting with Samira makes me feel more secure, especially since she is a head taller than I am, and twice my width. Judging from the stickers on her calendar, she belongs to a roller derby team, or something like that. If Jeremy and Caleb tried to bother me, she could strangle them with her thighs alone, they look that muscular.

The two of them minded their own business during class, probably because Mr. Lessard kept making funny comments, which had the other students laughing more than they do at their predictable insults. Mr. Lessard likes existential jokes and making fun of himself, often through incongruous comparisons. In an exercise with the sentence "coffee is black and bitter," he said his heart was exactly the same way.

When the bell rang, I leapt from my seat, eager to be the first out the door, to avoid the crowds in the stairway, and get home as quickly as possible. But Samira held me back.

"Wait for me, Ciel, we can leave together."

I waited for her, though I was a little afraid we would have to discuss Mr. Lessard's sense of humor again, which I find hilarious, but she doesn't appreciate. I was wrong. She wanted to know what my weekend plans were. I gave her a quick description of my projects, then we went our separate ways in the first-year students' hallway, since she had to get her backpack, and I was ready to leave. It worked out better than I thought, which was a surprise. I don't like feeling forced to interact with people. I always think I have nothing interesting to say, and that stresses me out.

Back home, I said "Hi" to my brother and João, who were playing Wii U in the living room, then I went to my room. Even though the system is outdated, they still love it. João has been Virgil's best friend since kindergarten. His family is Brazilian, like my father's. When he started school, he could hardly speak English, which meant that he and Virgil became best friends, since my brother speaks Portuguese very well, much better than I do. I never practice, except in the morning, when my father asks me, *Bom dia, como está?* I answer, *Estou bem, obrigada!* Virgil devours the Portuguese children's books that my father keeps on the living room shelves like a precious treasure. If he read as much in English, I wouldn't have to help him with his homework.

For the last twenty minutes, I have been lying on my bed. I stare at the ceiling instead of my phone. I haven't looked at it all day. I'm pretty sure I received new comments about my video, and I don't want the weekend to be ruined, since it's going to be boring enough as it is.

I close my eyes. My thoughts turn circles and leap from one subject to the next. I wonder if I shouldn't just delete my channel. Maybe it's too much. Why did I have to have this success now, at the beginning of the school year? I think about my new school. But really, I don't know what to think. I'm scared because everything familiar has disappeared. Everything is like a bad joke. And now Stephie wants to make new friends. That stresses me out too, because I'm afraid I'll say or do the wrong thing, and mess up her life. I don't want us to grow apart. She's my best friend, after all. With Eiríkur gone, and not even bothering to answer my messages, I'm pretty much alone. I wonder what Frank wants from me. He acted kind of strange in science. I wish Liam had asked me for my number. I'd really like to be his friend.

Then I hear João shout *"Merda!"* from the living room. Virgil gives a victory cry. I decide to close my eyes a minute....

♥ ♥ ♥

I wake up with a start when my phone starts vibrating on my bed. I glance toward the window. Still light outside. My father must not be back from work yet. By the time I find my phone in the covers, the person has hung up. I look to see who called. Stephie. Should I call her back? My mind is a little foggy from my unplanned nap, and all I feel like is going back to sleep. But I decide to call her. I'm happy she hasn't forgotten me.

"Hi! You called?"

"Yeah. What are you doing?"

"I fell asleep."

"That means I woke you up."

"More or less, yes."

"YES! One point for me."

I laugh. Stephie says, "I was wondering if you wanted to sleep over tonight."

"Aren't you with your mother on weekends?"

"I'm at my father's, and he says we can watch movies until two in the morning if we want!"

Stephie's parents separated when she was eight. I don't think they get along very well. According to her, they fight every time they see each other. She stays with her father one week out of two. I see her more often when she is at his place, since when she's at her mother's, they are always going out together.

I make a quick calculation. If I go to bed at two in the morning, I'll have three hours of sleep before having to get up to deliver the paper before six. That's not much. And if I deliver it too late, the doctor who gives me the big tips will not be so generous next week. But do I really need the extra money? I've saved almost all the money I need to buy the camera I have my eye on. Anyway, tomorrow is Saturday, so technically, I have until ten o'clock to deliver the paper. I can give myself a little break.

"That sounds great! When should I come?"

"Whenever you want. After dinner. Wait a second."

I hear her father talking.

"You want to eat at my place?" she asks. "My father's going to order Chinese."

I love Chinese food. My father isn't back yet, but I'm sure he won't mind if I sleep over at Stephie's, especially since João is with Virgil. And if I'm not there, they can speak Portuguese without worrying about me.

"Fine with me!"

"All right, my father's on the phone, ordering, so get over here fast!"

I hang up and breathe a sigh of relief. A great weight has been lifted from my shoulders. Stephie still wants to do things with me, even if she has plenty of new friends. All of a sudden, my fears seem absurd. How could I have thought that about Stephie? I burst into tears, but have to dry them fast so I can text my father and tell him I won't be eating at the house. Then I grab my bike and head for Stephie's father's place.

6

A Bad Week to Buy a New Car

Stephie's father is called Martin, and he's nice, even if he does make jokes and puns that sometimes aren't as funny as he thinks they are. At least he doesn't invade our space, not like my father, who thinks he's doing the right thing by bothering us every ten minutes to ask whether we need anything. Once we finish eating, we won't see Martin for the rest of the night. Usually, he disappears into his room until the next morning to build super-powerful computers and play video games on his PC with his brother. That's his one passion, and it's his job too, going to people's houses and businesses to fix their machines. Sometimes I wonder if he's disappointed that Stephie is completely uninterested in computers, especially since she is his only child.

The food shows up ten minutes after I do. There is a ton of rice, General Tso's chicken, chop suey, spareribs in garlic sauce, sautéed vegetables, and three fortune cookies, all waiting for us on the table.

Stephie begins making a list of what snacks she wants for our movie night. In the middle of it, her father asks me, "How's it going for you and high school, Ciel?"

"All right. The teachers aren't too bad."

"Stephie told me you're still delivering the paper in the morning. Is that hard with school?"

"I manage. I have to wake up before everyone else, so by the time school starts, I'm ahead of the game."

Stephie gives me a wink. "And when she goes home after school, she sleeps all afternoon."

"We'll see who stays awake until two in the morning!"

Martin smiles. "I wanted to ask you. Does your father still participate in those monthly meetings for parents of trans kids? I thought I might go next Tuesday."

Stephie almost chokes on her bean sprouts. She stares at her father in disbelief. Martin wants an answer. I can tell he's serious.

"I'm not sure, but I don't think so. I can ask him if he's planning on going, but I don't think he's been there for a year."

"Alice has been telling me about these meetings, and I'm thinking it might not be a bad idea." He smiles at Stephie, who is still staring at him, amazed. "But I'd feel more comfortable if I could go with someone I knew."

"I'll tell my father. Maybe he would go with you."

"That would be too cool, Dad, if you went with Gabriel," Stephie speaks up, clearly happy with the conversation.

It's incredible, the progress Martin has made since I've known him. When Stephie transitioned when she was nine, her mother was the one who supported her. Her father didn't take it very well, especially in the beginning. He went on using *he* when he talked about her, until she was ten, and he realized it wasn't just a phase. I don't think he was trying to be mean. He was just completely disoriented by everything that was happening. He even tried to get Stephie interested in football and Formula 1! Not that there's anything wrong with a girl liking those things. It's just the idea of pushing someone into certain activities in hopes of changing who they are—that's what I don't like. If my father had done that, I would have been really angry, and thought he didn't love me. It's a good thing Stephie is so stubborn and didn't listen to her father. Little by little, he must have understood that he was making her unhappy by trying to change the person she was.

When I compare my situation with Stephie's, I figure I'm lucky to have a father like mine, who has always supported and encouraged me. Even before he understood I was trans, he was willing to buy me books and clothes that were considered to be "for girls." The way my mother did, when she was still with me.

We finish most of the cartons of food, except for the chop suey that Martin is taking care of. Stephie and I each choose a fortune cookie. Mine reads, "It is a bad week to buy a new car," and Stephie gets, "Never listen to the advice of a brush salesman." Dazzled by the fortune-cookie wisdom, we put our plates and utensils in the dishwasher and disappear into Stephie's room.

I like being there. I always feel a sense of peace. A big window looks out on a leafy tree in her backyard, and the canary-yellow walls are decorated with Doctor Who posters, and pictures of actors from the musical *Lafontaine*, based on the life of Premier Louis-Hippolyte Lafontaine. I know the subject sounds boring, but the show is really good, and we love the music, the costumes, the whole thing. Stephie and I know all the songs by heart, from the first note to the last. For my birthday, two months from now, I asked my father for two tickets to the show. I'll invite Stephie—if she's still my friend. She should be interested, since Léonard Cadieux is playing the lead role, and even I think he's handsome.

Stephie sits down at her computer, and I crash out on the bed. She goes to her Netflix account.

"What do you want to watch?"

"I don't know. A horror film?"

"We didn't finish the paranormal series last time."

"That's true. But I wouldn't mind watching *Mean Girls* again."

"Me neither. We can watch both, no problem, since we have until two in the morning."

Mean Girls is our cult film. We must have watched it two dozen times. It's about a teenage girl who pretends to be popular so she can join the group that's terrorizing everyone at their high school. It's really too funny! Actually, it's not that funny, since we know all the lines perfectly, but I always like seeing it again.

"Did Eiríkur ever write back to you?" Stephie asks me as she navigates through Netflix.

"I would have told you if he had."

"You're too nice. If Frank acted like that with me, I'd be furious."

"I know he's not trying to hurt me," I answer. "The next time he writes back, I'll tell him I don't want to wait that long anymore, and he has to make more of an effort."

Stephie sighs, then comes and sits down on the bed next to me.

"Ciel, tell me the truth. Do you still love him?"

I think about it a few seconds.

"Yes…I think so. It's hard to say."

"That's a bad sign."

I sit up stiffly. I don't much like her comment.

"Not at all! What I mean is that we talk to each other so rarely, it's like he's not there anymore."

"He isn't there anymore," Stephie reminds me.

"He's still there. He's just a little far away."

"Think about it, Ciel," she tells me, teasing. "If you're single again, you can go out with that cute guy in our French class."

I pretend not to know who she means.

"What are you talking about?"

"You know very well *who* I'm talking about. The boy you keep staring at, the guy who was in the newspaper."

"Liam? I don't stare at him! And he doesn't interest me. He's just a little…mysterious."

I feel my cheeks turning red as I say the word. Stephie can't help but notice.

"Really? Can you tell me exactly what's so mysterious about him?"

"Lots of things. The fact that he's a national swimming champion, and he's never said a word about it. And that he's trans, but we've never seen him at the LGBT+ Youth Center. And that he seems to disappear between classes."

"Exactly what I thought. You're in love with him."

"Stop that!"

I throw a pillow at her head.

She starts laughing.

"Don't worry, I'm just bugging you."

"You're awful!"

Stephie throws the pillow back. "All right, I'll leave you alone. For the time being, at least. Come on, let's go to the store and buy some junk food."

There are two *depanneurs* near Stephie's father's place. The closest one is on Rosemont Boulevard, but it's small, and the other is on Beaubien, two blocks farther, but with better choice and lower prices. We decide to go to the one on Beaubien. We'll get some exercise, and besides, we don't have that much money.

On the way, I show Stephie the picture I took of the Gender and Sexuality Alliance poster.

"See that? The meeting is next Tuesday, at lunch. I figured I'd go."

"I didn't even know there was a LGBT club at school."

"Me neither, until I saw the poster. It was on the bulletin board by the cafeteria."

"I'm not sure I want to be seen at that kind of meeting," Stephie admits.

"Why not? You don't have to say you're trans. Just say you're there to support me as an ally."

"What if I'm the only ally there?" Stephie objects. "That would look strange. People would suspect something."

Her reaction makes me a little sad, even if I'm not exactly surprised. I suppose the meeting is one of those activities she has to avoid if she doesn't want to be perceived as the school's "trans girl."

"I guess I'm disappointing you," Stephie says softly.

"A little. You'll have to buy me a great big chocolate bar to get back in my good books!"

She elbows me, and almost knocks me into the gutter on Beaubien Street in front of the store. The clerk greets us as we enter. We head straight for the chip aisle, and begin to debate about what kind we want, then choose the same flavor we always go for, cottage cheese and pickle. It sounds disgusting, but for some reason it's good. While we're at it, we pick up a bag of jujubes and two chocolate bars. To wash it all down, we grab a two-liter bottle of cream soda, since the last time we got Orangeade. That's what Stephie likes, and I want cream soda, so we switch off. The clerk stuffs our gourmet selection into two plastic bags, and we head out the door.

In the parking lot next to the store, we cross paths with a group of teenage boys, older than we are, going toward the door. One of them yells at me as he goes past.

"Hey, look here! It's the little faggot from YouTube who doesn't know which bathroom to use!"

"Didn't your teacher make you feel extra special with your made-up gender?" his friend adds.

They burst out laughing as they pile into the store. My face turns as red as a tomato. My throat is tight, and I pretend I didn't understand, though Stephie heard every word. We start walking down Beaubien in silence. My hands are cold and trembling so hard I can barely hold the bag with the cream soda.

Stephie breathes out noisily, as if she had been holding her breath. But she still doesn't look at me.

"Are you okay?"

"So-so."

"They're disgusting. Don't listen to them. They don't even know you."

"They seemed to know me very well."

She doesn't answer. She seems to be thinking things over. The sun has just about set by the time we reach her father's place. She takes my arm before we go inside.

"I'm sorry, I should have spoken up for you. I'm no good as a friend."

I look her in the eye. I can feel her regret.

"No, that would have been worse. They would have bugged you, too."

"I should have done something instead of walking away without a word. I was afraid for myself, even though they were attacking you. I was selfish."

I shift the bag with the cream soda to my other hand, so I can take Stephie's.

"You shouldn't be mad at yourself. It's my fault. I'm the one who splashed their life all over the Internet."

"Stop that!" my friend orders me. "What you did with your video is very important, and you know it! Nobody else here will talk about the things you do. Even I won't do it anymore."

I don't know what to say. The soft twilight breeze brushes my arm and makes me shiver. I look down at my feet. I didn't know that Stephie felt bad about not being openly trans at school. I want to take my best friend in my arms. Instead, I look into her face. Her eyes are wet with tears. There are no words for this. We go into her house.

♥ ♥ ♥

Lying on our stomachs on Stephie's bed, surrounded by a giant bowl of chips, a torn-open bag of candy, and empty chocolate bar wrappers, we watch a few episodes of the paranormal series, including the one about an average American family that moves into a haunted house full of Tyrolian singers. Then we launch into *Mean Girls*, our absolute favorite. It's not like we're young kids, but it's after midnight, and Stephie is dropping off to sleep. She laughs at everything I say about the film, funny or not, and when I invent dialogue with the characters' voices.

She ends up falling asleep, her head on my shoulder. It feels good to me. I lay my cheek on her hair and watch the film to the very end. Then, as carefully as possible to keep from waking her, I slip my phone out of my pocket. I turn it on and write a quick message.

Her phone goes off, and she wakes up with a start. Her eyes full of sleep, she reaches for it on her bedside table. She squints at what's written there, then reads it out loud.

> *One point for me!*

I start laughing. When she hits me with a pillow, I laugh even harder.

7

Too Bad for Eiríkur

When I open my eyes, it's 8:58, but I let the alarm on my phone ring at 9 so Stephie will wake up. I'm in someone else's house, too shy to make myself breakfast on my own before heading out to deliver the paper.

I get dressed fast as Stephie drags herself to the bathroom. She comes into the kitchen. Her father isn't up yet, so we are as quiet as we can manage.

"What do you want to eat?" she asks, opening the cupboards. "There's bread and cereal, and I can make pancakes."

"I don't have time for pancakes. What kind of cereal do you have?"

"Frosted oat flakes."

"Maybe not. I'll have some toast."

Stephie puts two slices of bread in the toaster and serves herself a bowl of cereal.

"Want some juice?"

"I'd love some."

I spread caramel and jelly on my toast, then devour both pieces, washing them down with orange juice. While I'm at it, I dip into a bowl of cashews Martin left on the table. Stephie is so sleepy she can scarcely remember to put milk on her cereal. I wonder if it's safe to leave her alone and go deliver the paper. Maybe I should stay, in case she falls asleep in her bowl and drowns in the milk. But time is running out. I put my plate and my glass in the dishwasher, then give Stephie a big hug, in hopes of waking her up a little.

I pedal home as fast as I can. Instead of parking my bike at the back of the building, I lock it to the fence in front, to save time. I run up the metal stairs two by two, then jump over the pile of papers that the delivery truck left there a few hours earlier.

In the front hall, on the rug, I spot a pair of shoes I don't recognize. They must belong to João, who probably stayed over, since Virgil is a little copycat, and if I sleep over at a friend's, he has to invite someone over to do the same. Well, big deal. João is a nice kid, but Virgil is just too predictable.

I bring my newspaper bag into the hallway and cut

the plastic ties that keep the bundle together, then stuff the papers into my bag for delivery. Just then, my phone starts vibrating in my pocket. A message from Eiríkur! My heart is beating fast.

I'm late for my route and halfway out the door, so I'll read his message when I get back. Just to know that he wrote is good enough. I imagine his voice, and the strange way he pronounces "u" and "s." I am smiling to myself. *Let's go, get a move on!* I sling the delivery bag over my shoulder and go down the stairs to my bike. I head off on my route, pedaling on a cloud.

When I finish, I lock my bike in the backyard and go in through the kitchen door. Virgil and João are sitting at the table, eating breakfast. I go by with a quick hello and rush into the living room to read Eiríkur's email on the computer. Yes, I know, I could read it on my phone, but my little ritual lets me draw out the pleasure longer, since I have to turn on the computer. Behind me, my father is picking up the mess my brother and his friend left.

"Hi, there, cutie-pie! How was it at Stephie's?"

"Great! But we went to bed pretty late. And I got up early to deliver the paper on time."

"I saw that. You left the plastic straps in front of the door. But don't look for them, I put them in the garbage."

"Sorry, Dad."

I sit down in front of the computer, on the office chair. My father doesn't like that very much.

"Before you go on the machine, sort your dirty clothes. I'm going to do a wash."

"But, Dad! Eiríkur finally answered my email. I want to write back right away. I'll take care of my clothes after, okay?"

My father looks unhappy. He puts his hand on my shoulder.

"Sweetie, he made you wait for nearly two weeks. I can imagine how excited you are, but you shouldn't feel obligated to answer him immediately."

"I don't feel *obligated.*"

"I really have to do the wash, right now. Myriam and Leah are coming over for dinner tonight, remember? I'd like the house to be clean. Bring me the clothes you want washed, please. The sooner we finish the housework, the sooner we can go out for a ride."

I sigh, then get up. After all, I'm the one who wanted to go on a bike hike to Île de la Visitation, on the northern edge of the city. This might be the last weekend when it will be warm enough to go riding. I'll keep using my bike until November, maybe December, but Virgil gets cold, and doesn't want to be out when it's below fifteen degrees. My brother bugs me sometimes, but I still like to do things as a family. Since my father works hard, and Virgil is old enough to do things on his own, it's not very often that the three of us are all together at once.

I go to my room, promising to sort through my dirty clothes. But as soon as I close the door, I can't help myself. I pull my phone from my pocket and jump onto the bed to read Eiríkur's email. Too bad for my little ritual!

Subject: Re: Re: Re: Re: Re: Re: Re: Hello <3

Dear Ciel of my heart,

I hope you are fine. I'm sorry that it took me so long to answer your last email, school stole all my energy. I love you a lot too, and miss you. I finally saw your new video. A nice day in Maisonneuve Park! When I watched the video, I thought of the picnic we had with Frank and Stephie last year. Do you remember?

It's sad what happened in your French class, and

Ciel

I hope you worked things out with your teacher. On my first day of school, I told everyone I was bisexual when I introduced myself. Some people made remarks, but things went pretty well. The school is small, everyone knows each other, it's very different from Montreal. I like it when there aren't so many people.

I thought you were very beautiful in the video. In the sunlight, your hair looked very soft, and I wanted to run my hands through it.

I've played the Zelda game a lot this last week. It's one of the best. I did some drawings of Link during my classes. I'm going to put them on DeviantArt over the weekend, so you can see. I made a new friend at school, her name is Hilga, she likes drawing too.

If you like, we can talk on Skype this week. I'll ask my parents if I can stay up later.

Can't wait to see you!

Love and kisses,
Eiríkur

My father knocks on the door.

"Are you getting there, Ciel?"

"Coming!"

I put my phone on my pillow, get up from my bed, and hurry to gather up the pile of dirty clothes on the floor. A small mountain of beige, white, and black things. All I've worn since school started. Boring colors so I won't be noticed. I glance into my closet through the open door. All my colorful things are there, the flowered prints and leopard spots and spangles. All of a sudden, I've become so bland. That's not who I am. I pick up the heap of dirty clothes and promise myself that, next week, there will be more color in the pile.

João's mother comes to pick him up around eleven, and my father asks me to make the sandwiches and organize the snacks while he does a last load of laundry. A final expedition with the vacuum cleaner, and we're ready to go.

I decided to wait and not answer Eiríkur now. My father is right, my boyfriend can be patient too. After our bike trip, I'll have more time, and be able to concentrate better.

We head off, destination Île de la Visitation, about

forty-five minutes by bike from our house, if we keep to Virgil's pace. It's one of my favorite parks, an island in the Rivière des Prairies, with two old mills that look as if they're haunted.

It's warm, but the sky is cloudy, which is perfect for biking. Once we reach the island, we find a picnic table in decent enough shape, and sit down to eat. I remember the last time we came here, in July, the place was swarming with mosquitoes. It was impossible to bite into a sandwich without ending up with a mouthful of bugs biting back. If you add the ones we swallowed on our bikes, we must have eaten a complete meal. But this time of year, either they are hiding, or the birds have eaten them all, so there's no danger of them pestering us.

My father takes out the lunch from his saddlebags, and we attack our chicken salad sandwiches.

As I finish mine off, I remember what I promised Stephie's father last night.

"Dad, Martin wants to know if you'd go with him to the parents of trans kids meeting this week."

"Martin wants to go?" my father says, surprised. "Now, that's news. What day is it?"

"Tuesday, I think."

"I'll see. I'll call him this evening or tomorrow. Do you know why he wants to go?"

"I think Stephie's mother talked him into it."

"I'm glad he's listening to her for once."

Martin and my father don't have much in common, besides each being the parent of a trans child. Once, when he came to get me at Stephie's, my father heard Martin talking about her, and calling her by her birth name. That happened two years ago, but my father still hasn't gotten over it. He's stuck there. Why would someone call another person by a name they hate and have rejected, except to be mean, or refuse to accept that person? And, worse, do it behind their back? Luckily, Martin has gotten better about it since.

After we finish eating, we pack up everything, then tour the island before getting back on our bikes. It's all uphill to our house, but we manage to return before four o'clock. Just as well, since the sun is coming out from behind the clouds, and beating down on our shoulders. I'm soaked with sweat by the time I reach our door, and though I want to answer Eiríkur more than anything else, I head for the shower. That will give me some time to think about what I want to say.

Still, I have to move fast. Myriam, my father's colleague, and her daughter Leah are coming over for dinner. Leah is sixteen, older than I am. The last time she visited, we ended up having a contest to see who could make Virgil laugh hardest. I didn't like that very much. I felt she was trying to steal my position as his sibling. Besides, she has this style, very haughty and all, treating me like a child. And when our parents aren't around, she always manages to call me "he." But my father and her mother like each other a lot, so I do my best to put up with Leah. Luckily, our parents are too busy to see each other very often. I wouldn't want to have her around all the time.

I choose a dress with black lace around the collar and sleeves, and a dark gray jacket that gives me a casual look. Not bad! I decide to take a selfie and send it when I write to Eiríkur later on. I want the photo to be perfect, so I put on makeup. Mascara on my lashes, and the finishing touch, lip gloss and cheek definition. Might as well go all-out, and besides, I might even impress Leah.

Once I have a photo that I like (I had to take a hundred!), I sit down at the computer in the living room, and go onto my email. Then I hear the spring-popping noise my phone makes, telling me I have a new message. Who could be texting me? I don't recognize the number.

How's it going?

Okay. Who is this?

> *Frank*

I forgot I had given him my number. I add his name to my contacts.

> *Are you busy?*

> *Not really...I just got back from a bike ride*

> *Cool. Can I call you?*

> *Now?*

> *Now*

We have known each other for years, but this is the first time he wants to talk to me on the phone. His request is hard to refuse, though I would much rather write Eiríkur before Myriam and Leah come over. For more privacy, I go back to my room and lie down on the bed, then answer *Okay*. A second later, my phone rings.

"Hello?"

Frank's familiar voice flows into my ear.

"Hello, Ciel, how are you doing?"

"Greenhouse gases are heating up the planet and

melting the glaciers, which means that Montreal will soon be under water, but besides that, everything's cool. What about you?"

"I'm all right. Except for Montreal being under water, I guess. How's your weekend?"

"Stephie and I watched movies all night, last night."

"She told me."

In the silence, Frank is figuring out what to say, and how to say it. I wonder why he called. I'd be surprised if he just wanted to see how I was doing, or talk about global warming.

"Actually, I'm calling you…it's a little embarrassing. I'm calling you because I have some questions. They're probably stupid, but I'm afraid to ask Stephie. I'm afraid of hurting her feelings."

"If you're afraid of hurting her feelings, it's a good sign they're the wrong questions."

"I know. That's why I'm calling you."

This is like a game. I appreciate Frank, so I'm willing to answer his questions, but I don't mind having a little fun at the same time.

"Go ahead and ask," I tell him. "But I can't promise I'll answer."

"Thanks, you're a friend."

"We'll see if I'm still your friend once I've answered."

He laughs nervously. "Okay. First, I wondered if the

medication Stephie is taking is going to make her have her period."

"When you say 'the medication she's taking,' do you mean the hormone blockers or the hormone treatment she's going to start in a few weeks?"

"Uh…both."

"There is no medication that will make someone grow a uterus."

"What?"

"The uterus is what causes people to menstruate."

"Really?"

"Really. We had a class about that last year. If you were paying attention, you heard that only people who have a uterus can menstruate. I don't have one, and as far as I know, Stephie doesn't either and neither do you."

"You bet I don't," Frank assures me. "Okay, another question…. These medications, they keep you from having a beard, right?"

"Among other things, yes."

"Because we're the same age, and since I'm starting to grow a beard, I was wondering—"

I interrupt him. "If she did have facial hair, I think she'd shave. But that's her choice."

Silence on the other end of the line. I can tell he's worried.

"You know, she wouldn't be any less a girl if she had a beard like a Viking, or an Adam's apple, or a low voice."

"But it would be a little weird."

"Why?"

"People might think I was going out with a guy, or something."

I can't believe my ears. I wonder what he is even doing with Stephie.

"And that would be a real tragedy, right?"

"That's not what I mean! Some of my friends say I'm gay because I'm going out with Stephie, and I don't care."

"Good."

"Anyway, thanks for answering my questions. If you want, we could get together after school sometime. That would be cool."

"Sure, why not?"

Then it's good-bye, and I hang up with a sigh. I'm happy that Frank is sensitive to Stephie, but I can't keep from thinking about my dream of a school where everyone would be trans. No, not just a school. An entire city with just trans people. Where no one would ever have to explain who they are, and why.

I go back to the computer to write my message to Eiríkur. But as soon as I click on the browser icon, I hear someone knocking on the front door. Myriam and Leah are here. I get up with another sigh.

Too bad for Eiríkur, I guess.

8

Bettie Bobbie Barton Is Bored (like me)

It's almost midnight and Virgil is dozing on the sofa, and finally Myriam and Leah find their way to the door. The evening wasn't too bad after all. While my father talked with Myriam and drank whiskey (what a smell!), Leah, my brother, and I played *Mario Kart*, one of the only video games Virgil can beat me at, and a board game Leah brought. We played with Borki, throwing paper balls that he would rush to retrieve. Leah said he tried to bite her, but I don't believe it, he would never do that.

I am so tired I can hardly stand up after last night, when I hardly slept at all, at Stephie's. My vision is a little fuzzy, and on the way to the computer, I trip over the coffee table. When he sees me turn on the screen, my father, busy picking up the mess we made in the living room, is not too happy.

"You really want to go on the computer at this hour of the night? You should get some sleep, sweetie."

He's probably right. I have to rub my eyes to tell one key apart from the other.

"But I have stuff to do!"

"You'll have all day tomorrow."

I decide to listen to him, since I'm about to pass out. But before I turn off the computer, I pay a quick visit to my YouTube account, in case there are new comments to delete. I haven't taken a peek for two days. I needed a little break. The last time, the number of people who had viewed my video stood at about eight thousand! Just thinking about that number made me dizzy, as if I were jumping off the Olympic Stadium tower on a bungee cord.

When I access my page, I nearly stop breathing. The number of clicks has almost doubled since Friday! I can hardly believe it. I never would have imagined that the little video I made in the park would create such a stir. It's exciting, but at the same time, I do feel like I've lost control. There are a lot of racist comments, stuff like "Go back to your own country," and "Don't come here and complain." My favorite one: "You should be happy to be in Quebec instead of Brazil, back there they wouldn't let you dress so badly." I don't bother to delete all of them, there are too many and I'm too tired. It's strange because in my video I never mentioned that my father is Brazilian, at least not in this one. And people seem to have an obsession with my hair. Apparently, the cream I used to smooth it down really had an effect.

I turn off the computer. I'll take care of the rest tomorrow. One last glass of water, then into the bathroom to brush my teeth and take off my makeup. A lot of times, I forget to do that. I read an article on the Internet that says it's really important not to skip that part—even if I don't remember why. I put on a lot today for the selfie I'll send Eiríkur. I can post it on Instagram and Snapchat, while I'm at it.

As I remove my makeup with a wipe, in the harsh light above the mirror, I notice the hair on my face. Most of it is like down. The few hairs that are thicker are light chestnut, like my eyes, so they're scarcely visible. I think back to the conversation with Frank, when he asked me if Stephie was going to grow a beard. I wonder what I'd look like if I had one. At school, some of the boys are starting to grow sketchy mustaches. Some even have hair on their necks. Pretty soon they'll have Viking beards!

A little voice inside me pipes up: *It would be funny to have a beard.* I could experiment, and see if I like it, and shave it if I didn't. Or do like that lady I met on Trans Pride day, back in August, who had her hair removed with a laser. They say it's really painful, and she didn't recommend it. All I would need is to stop taking hormone blockers for a few months, and presto! I'd have a little beard.

Every month, I go to the community health center in Saint Leonard for a hormone blocker injection. That's why I don't have facial hair, and why my voice hasn't started to change, like Frank's and Eiríkur's. Unlike Stephie, I haven't decided whether I want to follow the hormone treatments that are supposed to come next, that will make my breasts grow and my hips widen, the things that most cisgender girls want. To be honest, that doesn't really interest me. I only know I don't like the idea of my voice changing and my arms getting hairy like my father's. I have nightmares about that, so you get the picture.

I take one of the disposable razors my father bought me, and shave off the hairs on my cheeks, chin, and above my lip. Magic! My skin is as smooth as a baby's.

In bed, I rub the covers over my perfect skin, and decide there's no way I would want too much testosterone running through my veins. Not even to grow a Viking beard as a joke.

♥ ♥ ♥

It's drizzling when I deliver the papers on Sunday morning, which means I have to put them all in little plastic bags so they won't get soaked before people get around to taking them out of their mailboxes. It's extra work, and I don't get paid for it. Life is unfair sometimes. But the bad weather means the raccoons stay home, and that's good.

When I return home, it's still early. Everyone is sleeping, except Borki. Quietly, he comes to see who is there when I close the door. The time is finally right to answer Eiríkur's message. There is no one around to bother me. On this Sunday morning, I can't even hear the cars on Rosemont Boulevard.

I take my time and read his letter several times. I react to each thing he says, and ask for more information about certain details. I go on his DeviantArt profile, the site where he puts his drawings online, to check whether he uploaded the ones from *Zelda* that he said he did last week. Of course not, he's too lazy! I agree to talk on Skype this week. I miss his voice so much…. I suggest Wednesday evening, to leave him time to confirm. Late afternoon where I am, the end of the evening where he is, with the five-hour time difference between Montreal and Iceland.

I finish my message with a few of my recent adventures. My video that has been viewed almost sixteen thousand times, the comments on my channel over the last week, Stephie's girlfriends who are suddenly nice to me, Frank calling to ask me questions about her, the bike ride to Île de la Visitation. I mention the Gender and Sexuality Alliance meeting on Tuesday, where Stephie is supposed to go with me.

Before I send my email, I attach my favorite selfie from the ones I took yesterday. I'm smiling, my smile looks sincere, and my hair falls nicely onto my shoulders. I hit "Send." I can't wait to get his answer. If he really wants us to talk on Skype this week, he will have to write back faster than last time.

Before taking a shower and eating the breakfast my father is going to make when he gets up (on Sunday, he likes to make us eggs with potatoes and ham), I take a look at Instagram and Facebook. A few people have commented on the selfie I uploaded onto both sites this morning.

"Too cute!"

"♥♥♥"

"Bay-bee!"

"You'll go far with that smile!"

"You look just like your mother when she was your age."

The last comment comes from my Aunt Annie. She always makes me a little uncomfortable with her bad-taste jokes and embarrassing remarks, but this time, her words make me smile. I like the idea that I look like my mother when she was my age. Virgil looks more like my father with his coal-black hair.

Then I notice someone sent me a private message on WhatsApp. It's Benoît Vandroogenbroeck, a boy from Quebec City I met on a secret group for young trans people. Stephie signed me up a few months back. We don't really know each other, Benoît and I, but he loves my YouTube channel, and he always shares and comments on everything I post.

Benoît: Hey, Ciel, did you see this?

Benoît: https://www.youtube.com/287689739 eh3uodhedkjhkazs...

Intrigued, I click on the link. It's a video by Bettie Bobbie Barton, a trans girl of seventeen or eighteen, who lives in Guelph. She is pretty well known, and she uses her visibility to make videos criticizing trans people. Yes, I know, it doesn't make sense, but it does make her very popular with the audience that doesn't like trans people. People think she's pretty with her big blue eyes, her shiny blond hair, and her Barbie body. Apparently, that gives her the right to say anything she wants.

The title of her video? *Gender-special Latino-Brazilian starved for attention.* That doesn't sound good. My heart starts beating hard as I hit Play. Bettie Bobbie launches into a tirade, all smiles.

Hi, everybody! Today I watched a video that made me want to puke, about a gay boy who invented a gender for himself by saying he's neither a boy nor a girl. I guess he figures being Latino is not special enough. I grit my teeth and clench my fists. I feel like stopping the video, turning off the computer, forgetting about everything that's going on out there. But I need to know what she is saying about me. It's all I can do to keep listening.

In his video, he tells how his school has no special washroom for people who are neither boys nor girls. I think that's funny. You really have to be mixed up to imagine that society is going to accommodate every whim that a few weird people have, when all they want is more attention! I can't believe my ears. She made an entire video about me, she insults me in public, and I'm the one who needs attention?

Bettie Bobbie ends with a self-satisfied look.

If you ask me, this video harms real trans people like me, who have real problems, unlike the other kind who make up a gender for themselves that doesn't exist. I hope Ciel will go back to Brazil, and stop bothering us with his little whims, or at least cut his hair because, as you can see, it's a real pain to look at. Have a nice day! The video ends with a screen capture off my last video, chosen on purpose because it looks like I am making an ugly face.

The video was posted late Friday night, and it already has thirty thousand views. I feel myself blush. Thirty thousand people listened to this scrap heap of lies about me! At least now I know where all the racist comments I read last night come from.

Before thanking Benoît for sending me the link to the video, I quickly modify my channel to keep people from adding new comments, at least until the storm blows over. I click on a little box in the parameters. It won't let my friends write positive messages, but that's a sacrifice I'm willing to make.

Strange, but I don't feel down after watching the video. Quite the opposite. Bettie Bobbie noticed me and decided to attack me, which proves she's taking me seriously. Personally, I'd rather be the enemy of someone so hateful than her friend. She gave me tens of thousands of new viewers for my video, and that's not bad. And I have a hundred new subscribers to my channel.

Thank you, Bettie Bobbie!

I decide not to mention her to my father, because I know he'll try to convince me that I shouldn't have a YouTube channel. It's tough on him to read the comments I received on my last video, even if he tried to hide his feelings. Not that he doesn't encourage me when I have a project. On the contrary, he's just worried about my safety. I go out to deliver the paper every morning, and that's already dangerous enough for him. He's afraid something will happen to me when I'm on my bike all alone on the streets of Montreal at six in the morning. Except for a raccoon attack, I don't see any danger.

I send the link to Bettie Bobbie's video to Stephie. She hates BB with pure, crystal hatred. She writes right back.

> I hope you'll answer

> I don't know. A good idea, but I don't want to give her more attention

Because of Bettie Bobbie's video, I feel full of energy, and I'd like to use it to make a new video. But it has started raining harder than earlier this morning, so the park is off limits. I'm afraid I'm going to have to do my homework instead.

You're still thinking of going to the GSA meeting Tuesday?

Yes. Are you going to come?

You'll never guess what happened. Remember Zoe who eats with us?

Yes

I write *Yes*, but I'm not sure. Is she the one in English, or the one with the short hair?

She's looking for someone to go to the GSA meeting with her. She doesn't want to be the only straight ally.

Ha ha! She thinks you're an ally too?

I guess so

I don't think she knows I'm trans

What did you tell her?

That I was going to be there 😉

So you're going to come?

Yep!

Hurray!! 😃 😃 ♥ ♥

And here I thought Stephie wanted to avoid everything trans. I'm happy to see I was wrong.

9

You're Adorable, Jerome-Lou!

I fix my hair the best I can with a glance in our locker mirror, with the message "Too Cute!" there to buoy my spirits. Bettie Bobbie's comment about my hair is still running in my head. Maybe I should have put more cream on my comb this morning. I'm waiting for Stephie, to go to the Gender and Sexuality Alliance meeting. I'm not nervous at all. On the contrary, I'm excited, too excited almost, by the idea of being in a room full of people like me, here at school, instead of only once in a while at the Montreal LGBT+ Youth Group. I'm not trying to say that all LGBT+ people are the same, but we're a little like family. Though we're all different, we have had similar experiences, and we can understand and help each other without having to explain ourselves or being afraid of rejection.

Stephie shows up, finally, with Zoe, who smiles at me. Before they have time to start talking, I quickly shut the locker door.

"We'd better hurry!" I tell them. "The pizza will be gone if we get there too late."

We start off in the direction of the meeting room at the other end of the world.

"I'm happy you're here too," Zoe says to me. "It's less intimidating for me with both of you."

"This is the only committee I'd get involved with."

"Why? Do you have LGBT people in your family?"

Suddenly, I feel embarrassed. I didn't know Zoe thought I was cisgender. I don't feel like explaining to her that I'm trans, especially not with Stephie here, who made me promise to avoid the subject. What should I do?

"Uh…not really."

"Don't worry, it's okay. I know." Then Zoe leans over and whispers, "You're a lesbian?"

Stephie and I share a secret look. It's not the first time one of us has been asked that. I give Zoe a wink. She smiles back.

"Don't worry, I won't tell anyone!"

♥ ♥ ♥

A couple dozen students fill the room. The place looks like a coiffure club. Half the people have their hair dyed some fluorescent color: green, pink, blue, turquoise. I'm pretty ordinary with my natural color, though maybe I'm too easily influenced.

A man greets us, inviting us to serve ourselves from the table where several boxes of pizza are set out. Luckily, there is enough to feed a whole herd. And I like the choices.

"There's even vegetarian. Too cool!"

That one is perfect for me, with its mountain of broccoli, squash, zucchini, and eggplant. Zoe must think I'm a little too enthusiastic.

"Are you a vegetarian?" she asks.

"No. But it sure looks good."

Zoe wrinkles up her nose, and reaches for the pepperoni and cheese variety. We each take two slices, then find a free spot to eat. Zoe talks with Stephie, and I check out the room in case there are people I know.

That's when I notice Liam. I'm surprised. It's the first time I've seen him outside my French class. He's by himself, near the window, in his own world. His earphones are clamped securely over his ears, and he's munching on a vegetarian slice, like me. I want to go over and ask him if he thinks it's good. But I don't know if that's the right way to start a conversation. He might think I'm weird if I interrupt him to talk about vegetables.

"Ciel? Hey, Ciel!"

I turn around. Stephie is trying to get my attention. A person with blue hair is standing in front of us, looking at me curiously.

"Hi! Sorry, I didn't mean to disturb you."

"No problem!"

Stephie looks at me suspiciously.

"What—or who—were you watching?"

"Nothing. My mind was just wandering."

The student with the blue hair tells me, "I wanted to say I love your videos. What you're doing is really good. I didn't know you were in school here."

I immediately start blushing, and stammer out a thank you. The person goes back to their friends before I have the chance to say anything more. Stephie elbows me in the ribs.

"See, you're a star!"

"What videos?" Zoe wants to know.

"I have a YouTube channel. Nothing too extraordinary."

"Nothing too extraordinary? Don't be so modest. People here recognize you! You'll have to send me the link. I'll go watch."

I laugh, twice as embarrassed, but promise Zoe I'll give her the information. The man who greeted us when we came in calls for silence so he can speak. He is an older man, almost bald, with wrinkles around his mouth that straighten out when he smiles.

"Oh, my God! There are so many of you! I don't remember having so many people at an Alliance meeting since we founded the group back in 2001. Most of you know me, but I'll introduce myself for the new students. My name is Guy. I've been in charge of student affairs at the school since...oh, my God, the last twenty-five years. In my position, I coordinate the different groups and committees, such as the student orchestra, the hockey team, the Dungeons and Dragons committee."

"There's a Dungeons and Dragons committee?" Stephie whispers loudly.

"If you want the complete list of committees," Guy goes on, "just look in the back of your school calendar. Of course, I don't personally look after every group, but I make an exception for the Gender and Sexuality Alliance, since it has a special place in my heart. You'll see, the things that happen here are magic! Feel free to come and see me if you have questions or ideas for activities, or if you want to talk about something—even if it's your dog or your cat. My office door is always open. Room B-1011. No need to write it down, it's in your calendar too. Now, with no further ado, I hand the meeting over to the Alliance president, Jerome-Lou de la Chevrotière."

"Oohs" and "ahhs" break out across the room, and calls of "You're adorable, Jerome-Lou!" A tall, slender student, wearing a freshly pressed black shirt and a pink tie, rises to take over from Guy, who goes and sits behind the pizzas.

"Thank you, Guy, and hello, everybody!" Jerome-Lou welcomes the room energetically. "I'm happy to see so many faces I know, and just as many that I don't. I hope this will be the start of a great year. As Guy told you, I am the Alliance president, and have been since last November. I've been at this job for nearly a year, and I must say, it has been such a great experience I'm considering running in the next election. I hope you'll all vote for me! Ha-ha! Seriously, the president's job is to coordinate the different activities of the Alliance, and make sure the meetings run well. Since this is the first one of the year, we'll take it easy. We don't want to scare off the newcomers. Ha-ha! I'm not a one-man team, there's Maxence—raise your hand, Maxence—the treasurer, and Marine, our vice-president. She'll take my place if I'm assassinated. Ha-ha! Today, we're going to go around the room so everyone can introduce themselves.

Say your name and something about yourself. Like your favorite band, for example."

I immediately raise my hand. Jerome-Lou looks at me, encouraging.

"Yes? A question?"

"Can we also say the pronouns we want people to use with us?"

"Excuse me? What pronouns?"

"For the person's gender. He/him/his, she/her/hers, they/them/theirs...."

When I started questioning my gender, it was very important to have a choice when it came to the pronouns people used with me. I needed space to discover the person I was. Until then, I would have never dared to ask people to say "they" when they talked about me. A lot of people imagine that transitioning is like waking up one morning and changing your entire life—your appearance, your habits, your preferences. But, really, it's allowing yourself the freedom to explore who you are and could be.

Obviously, Jerome-Lou doesn't agree. He laughs, then answers, "We don't want to turn the Alliance into a grammar class."

A few people echo his laughter. I lower my eyes, ashamed. I bitterly regret having brought up the subject. Then the person with the blue hair speaks up.

"Actually, it's not about grammar. It's a common practice in a number of LGBT+ groups. We want everyone to feel respected and free to experiment, and the Alliance should be there to do just that. We can't guess people's genders just from their appearance."

A number of people in the room nod in agreement. Even Liam emerges from his private world to support my proposal. Suddenly I'm proud of myself.

"All right, we can do that if you like. Say your name, your favorite band, and your pronouns. I'll start. You know my name, Jerome-Lou. My favorite band is Five Seconds of Summer. And, as you can probably guess, I prefer masculine pronouns. Ha-ha!"

Right then, I know I could never trust Jerome-Lou.

I listen carefully to every student's introduction, even if I realize that with my terrible memory for names and faces, I'll forget everything by the time the meeting is over. When it's my turn, I say my name is Ciel, that my pronouns are they/them/theirs, and that my favorite band isn't really a band, but a musical, *Lafontaine*. I'm happy to see that some people know it and approve of my choice, and that fills me with pride a second time.

Then Stephie says her name, and that she uses she/her/hers. But she stumbles when it comes to her favorite band.

"Hmm…. It's hard to say. I think that, well, I like *Lafontaine* too."

I know it's ridiculous, but it breaks my heart when she hesitates. We've been listening to nothing but *Lafontaine* for the last two years. I wonder if she's beginning to think it's immature. I don't want to have to find someone else to see the show with, in a month or two. It wouldn't be the same. But maybe I'm reading too much into things, as usual.

The introductions keep coming. When it's Liam's turn, he mentions a group I've never heard of, but I promise myself to look it up later. To end that part of the meeting, Guy, who was sitting quietly at the pizza table, gets up to introduce himself again, with his pronouns and favorite group (The Beatles).

"For the rest of the time," he tells us, "you can talk among yourselves, and have more pizza—there's plenty—and Jerome-Lou and I are going to circulate and answer your questions and get to know you. For next week, think of some activities you'd like to do during the year. That will be the subject of the meeting."

The room is getting really noisy, too noisy for me. I summon my courage and go see Liam. I always talk too fast when I'm nervous, but I manage not to trip over my words.

"Hi. Listen, I know I'm a little late, but I wanted to congratulate you for your gold medal at the Canadian Swimming Championships."

Liam smiles. "Thanks. Really, it wasn't much. The name is pompous, the competition isn't that difficult."

"But difficult enough for you to make page one of the newspaper!"

"Oh, no, don't tell me you saw that," he says, frowning.

"I did, sorry. The photo was cool."

"Right! A photo of me in a swimsuit on page one of the biggest paper in Montreal. You're the first person to mention it. Do you read the paper?"

"A little. I have a job delivering it, and sometimes I page through."

"That sounds great."

"More or less. It's repetitive and I have to wake up early. I'm saving to buy a video camera for my YouTube channel."

"You have a channel? Me too. What's yours called?"

"*Ciel Is Bored.* I made a video about trans people not too long ago."

Liam looks surprised. Apparently, he just realized that I'm trans, like he is. Funny, I would have thought he knew right away. He takes out a piece of paper and writes down the name of my channel.

"I can't wait to see it."

"Okay, but don't look at all the comments. Bettie Bobbie just posted a pretty vulgar response to my last video, and there's plenty of nonsense in the comment section I haven't had time to delete."

"Who did you say?"

"Bettie Bobbie Barton."

"I don't know her."

Just then, the Honorable President Jerome-Lou heaves into view and interrupts our conversation.

"You're talking about Bettie Bobbie? I find her delectable. Excellent, even. Ha-ha!"

Liam doesn't answer, and I am completely stunned. Our reaction doesn't seem to bother Jerome-Lou. He offers his hand to shake, as if we were at a spaghetti supper, and he was raising money for a political party.

He asks us to repeat our names.

"So happy to meet you!" he exclaims. "You'll come to our next meeting?"

Liam and I nod without much conviction, hoping he'll disappear as quickly as possible. He shakes our hands again, then goes off to victimize other people. A creepy feeling runs down my spine as I watch him.

Liam stares at him in disbelief, then turns to me.

"Are you on WhatsApp?"

10

The Worst Cameraman in Town

My father hesitated until the last minute, but on Tuesday evening, he finally decided to go with Stephie's father to the parents of trans people meeting. I have gone several times, since parents often bring their children, and they play in the room next door, but now I'm too old for that. One of the group leaders told me, if I wanted, that I could run a workshop for kids, but that's really not my cup of tea. I'm afraid something will happen while I'm there looking after them. Stephie is better than I am, since she babysits sometimes. The group leader should have asked her.

We eat dinner earlier than usual so my father can get downtown for the meeting by six. Of course, he can't leave without giving us a list of what to do—and what not to.

"There's some leftover cake on the white plate, serve yourselves. And be good! I should be back by nine. If you need to, you can always text me."

"Yes, Dad."

He kisses us, then hurries out the door.

Myriam brought over the pineapple and lavender cake last Saturday, but it was much too big to finish all at once, so we've been having it for dessert every evening since. When the cat's away, the mice will play. I cut Virgil an enormous slice, which he drowns in his glass of milk. That's his favorite way of eating dessert. The cake drinks up the milk and turns into a wet glob of dough, a kind of cake soup. Personally, I prefer my milk on the side, but to each their own.

We stack our dishes in the dishwasher, Virgil settles in front of the TV to play the latest *Zelda* game, and I turn on the computer. We had time to film my new video before dinner—inside, since it has been raining all day—and I want to finalize it as quickly as possible. It will be my answer to Bettie Bobbie.

Before getting down to work, I go on WhatsApp and search for Liam Johnson's profile. He doesn't use his real name. His pseudonym is Eugene Leroux, his cat's name, or so he said. I have no trouble finding him, and I send him a friend request.

A few minutes later, I receive a notification telling

me Liam has accepted my request. I see that he's online. My fingers hesitate on the keyboard a moment, and I wonder if I should send him a message now or wait. Go for it, I decide.

Ciel: Hello.

Which I immediately regret, because it's not original in the slightest. I should have put exclamation marks, or at least an emoticon. He must think I'm really boring. A minute or two later, he answers.

Liam: Hey, hi, Ciel! How's it going?
Ciel: Fine, you?
Liam: I'm still trying to get over the meeting this noon.
Ciel: Really? 🙁
Liam: Just kidding.
Liam: But it was pretty bad.
Ciel: Especially Jerome-Lou.
Ciel: Good day, my royal subjects, before you stands your lord. Today I have come to bestow my light upon you. Such an opportunity you have to bask in the presence of my adorable incandescence!

Liam: Ha-ha-ha!
Ciel: "Ha-ha-ha!" is right! You may kiss my hand. Please don't faint dead away in the face of my magnificence!
Liam: LOL OMG
Liam: You're too much!

I smile, happy that he thinks I'm funny. I feel a little bad about caricaturing Jerome-Lou like that, but it's too tempting, considering how pretentious he is. And it helps me get over my shyness. I'm afraid I'll bug Liam if I write too much. What if he's only answering to be polite? I decide to wait for him to send the next message, instead of monopolizing the conversation. No worries—he starts writing.

Liam: You think you'll go back next week?
Ciel: Really, I'm not sure. My girlfriends wanted to go, so maybe. You?
Liam: I'm not sure either. There won't be pizza next time, and I don't feel like making a lunch.
Ciel: What do you usually do for lunch?
Liam: I eat at home, I live right next to school.

Aha! The cat is out of the bag! That's why I never see him in the cafeteria. Okay, it wasn't one of the world's great mysteries, but still, I was wondering.

Liam: Hey, I can't find the paper where I wrote the name of your YouTube channel. What is it?

I blush, there in front of my screen, which happens every time someone mentions my channel. I send him the link, so he won't have to search for it.

Liam: Thanks! I'll go watch as soon as I can.
Ciel: I didn't ask the name of yours.
Liam: It's nothing much, just some videos of computer games I play.
Ciel: That's okay. 😃 *I'll subscribe!*
Liam: Great.
Liam: It's Minecraftmontreal2005LJ.
Liam: Even if I don't play Minecraft much anymore.
Liam: Gotta go, I have swimming practice. Talk soon!
*Ciel: Bye! ^_^*

Liam is pretty special. We hadn't talked to each other before today at noon, he never says a word to anyone, but when we met, it was like we had known each other forever. I wonder if that's because we're both trans. Would he be so open with just anyone? I try and think back to his attitude before I mentioned my YouTube channel, before he understood I was trans too. I congratulated him on his gold medal. He seemed a little shy, but he smiled. Maybe he's nicer than he lets on.

I find his YouTube channel with no problem, despite his complicated name. I watch a number of short sequences of video games. The most recent one is two months old. It's not the kind of thing that interests me, but I think it's cool that he has something like that in his life. I subscribe to his channel, which increases his number of subscribers to nine, and play some of his most recent videos, then click on the little thumbs-up, to encourage him and boost the number of viewers. On the sofa, Virgil is getting impatient.

"Put on the headset!"

"I'm almost finished."

Since I'm on YouTube, I decide to clean up some of the comments I received on my channel, then deactivate them. Certain people seem to have watched all my videos just to write hurtful messages. A lot of them must have seen Bettie Bobbie's, since they mention my hair (which looks just fine, by the way) and my Brazilian background. It makes me feel defenseless. What can I do, except use my spare time to clean up the comment threads?

Once I finish, I get to work editing the short video Virgil and I filmed this afternoon. I put on the big headset we keep by the computer, so I won't disturb Virgil with the noise, but also to protect myself from his game's aggressive soundtrack.

"Hi! Ciel here, for *Ciel Is Bored*."

It's hard work, editing these videos. When I record, my voice always sounds like a quacking duck. Stephie tells me that everyone feels the same way about their voice, but I can't stand the sound. I need to work on improving my voice.

I go on editing.

"No, wait. I wasn't ready. Hi! Ciel here! No, that's not good. Um. Hi, Ciel here for *Ciel Is Bored!*"

Sometimes I just can't stand myself. The three takes were identical. I delete the first two, and sigh.

"First, I'd like to thank everyone for the support they have given me over the last week. It really means a lot to me."

Have I really descended into the realm of clichés? Can't I do better than that? I just freeze up in front of the camera. At the time, I didn't realize how bad I was. But I'll keep it, it's all I have.

"After I put up my last video, I had the pleasure of getting a response from another YouTuber, who accused me of not being a real trans person and doing this just to attract attention. On top of that, she told me to go back to Brazil. First of all, my father might be Brazilian, but I've only been to that country twice, as a kid. I don't know where she came up with that nonsense, but I have nothing more to say about it. Though if someone wants to buy me a ticket to Brazil, well, go ahead! Second, I have no quarrel with anyone. I don't have to prove that I'm a 'real' trans person. Trans people shouldn't have to prove to anyone that they're really the gender they identify with. That's impossible to prove! How could we do it? Give them a choice between playing with trucks or dolls? Ridiculous!"

"Burp!"

"I'm sure plenty of cisgender people would fail that test."

"Buuuurp!"

"Virgil? Did you just burp?"

"Do you think anyone could hear?"

"Of course! You're right behind the camera."

"Oops. Sorry!"

I pause the video and rub my eyes. I must have the

worst cameraman in town. Luckily, I don't have to pay him. Except with the ton of licorice he eats after every shoot.

♥ ♥ ♥

I spend forty-five minutes editing the video. I decide to put it on my channel tomorrow afternoon, so Eiríkur will be awake to see it. Right now, he must be sleeping. Unless he's playing *Zelda* in secret. He can do that, since he has a TV in his room. Last year, sometimes he would show up at school blinking his eyes, half-asleep, poor baby. He even snored in English class once. That never happens to me, and I wake up every morning at five-thirty.

I let out a sigh. It's crazy how much I miss him. Tomorrow I'm supposed to talk to him on Skype. But he hasn't confirmed our date. I sure hope he will soon. The last time we talked was August 22, three weeks ago. It was early in the morning and I was tired because of the time difference. Tomorrow, it will be the other way around. I'll call him when I get back from school, but it will be nine o'clock at night where he is. I don't know how much time we'll have to talk.

I waste a few more minutes on the Internet, looking at the latest funny stuff on Tumblr. I took off my headphones, and now I have to put up with the music from my brother's game. Time passes slowly. I'm waiting for Liam to come back from his swim practice. How many hours per week does a national champion dedicate to training? Or per day? He's already the champion, he shouldn't have to do too much more. An hour? Two? Can someone really spend two hours swimming without being completely exhausted?

Something on the screen makes me laugh out loud.

"What's that? What's going on?" my brother asks, keeping his eyes on his game.

"Just a dog rolling around in bubble wrap."

Virgil pauses his game and comes to take a look. He's always ready to look at funny dog videos.

"He looks just like Borki!"

I send the image to Stephie on WhatsApp, hoping to make her laugh, but she's not online. When she's at her mother's, they often go out in the evening, even during the week, to see a show, or read in a café with a cup of hot chocolate. I'm a little envious. That's the kind of activity I would have liked to do with my mother. She loved to read, and she used to take me to the library. I don't read much anymore, these days. It's like I never have the time.

When I think about my mother, I miss her. I decide to go into my room to try and change my mood.

I lie down on my bed, surrounded by a couple dozen stuffed animals. Then I come across the advertising flyer from the electronics store in the Galeries d'Anjou, the big shopping center fifteen minutes by bus from my house. The flyer was on my bedside table, and I start flipping through it. In the middle is the section with video cameras, and I see the model I want, on special, reduced to $409.99 from $529.99. My eyes open wide. I jump up and search for the little wooden box with the lock on it. That's where I keep the money I have saved from my paper route over the last few months. I've been too lazy to take it to the bank and put it into my account. I open the lock and empty the box onto my bed.

The camera is $409.99, and I have to add the tax, which would come to…. Why am I so bad in math? Maybe sixty dollars more? Then I'll need a tripod to mount the camera, so Virgil won't wobble the picture all over the place. Let's say I'll need something like five hundred and ten dollars. I have two forty in my bank account, so I'm missing about two hundred and seventy dollars. I start counting the money, making little heaps with the coins and piling up the bills. The sum comes to a hundred and eighty four, sixty-five. Which means I would need fifty-five dollars and thiry-five cents in tips this week. On Thursday, my customers are supposed to pay me. Usually they give me between forty and sixty dollars in tips, depending on the doctor who rewards me generously for delivering his paper before six in the morning.

Then I remember one fateful detail. I delivered the paper later last Saturday, after spending the night at Stephie's. Farewell, twenty-dollar tip from the rich doctor!

I could always wait a little before buying the tripod. It's not the end of the world if I don't get it at the same time as the camera. But it would be a real mistake not to buy the camera when it's on sale this week. The first page of the flyer clearly states that the discounts are valid until this Saturday. I'd like to go earlier, ideally Thursday evening, when I'll have the money I need. Worse comes to worse, I'm sure my father would lend me twenty dollars.

I'm so excited I feel like jumping up and down. I'll finally have my camera! And I won't have to deliver papers anymore. Too cool!

It's not even eight o'clock, but I decide to go to bed earlier than usual, so the doctor will have his paper before daybreak. Who knows, maybe he'll forgive me for having delivered it late last Saturday.

I say good night to Virgil, who is still glued to the television screen, then brush my teeth, set my alarm for 4:30 a.m., and go off to bed with a smile.

♥ ♥ ♥

At 4:28, when I wake up, the rain has stopped. I'm not usually up this early. The sky is pitch black and there isn't a single bird singing, just a few cars with their motors rumbling on the wide boulevard the next block over.

I open the front door to see whether my pile of papers has arrived. Not yet. Only the heavy, humid city air, colder than I imagined it. A mistake to have awoken this early. There's no use if I don't have the papers to deliver. I go back to my room to wait for the truck, and close the door so I can turn on my light without disturbing my brother, since his room is right next to mine. He leaves his door open so Borki can come and go, but as soon as there is any light, he wakes up. It's not very convenient.

I reach for my phone. All kinds of messages came in while I was sleeping. First, an email from Eiríkur, a very short one, confirming our Skype date for this evening. I answer him quickly: "Great! Talk to you soon. Can't wait to see you. ♥ *Ég elska þig!*"

Ég elska þig means "I love you" in Icelandic. He taught me that. The letter þ is hard to find on my phone, it's called "thorn" and pronounced a little like "th," but more complicated. Icelandic is not my strongest subject.

I have some WhatsApp messages too. Around ten

p.m., Stephie finally saw the picture of the dog in the bubble wrap, and she answered "LOL." I don't know if I should respond. That was seven hours ago; it's a little late, but I send an emoticon sticking out its tongue.

I'm happy to see that Liam, who must have come back from his swim practice around ten-thrty, sent me a dozen WhatsApp messages.

Liam: I'm back now, I'll look for your channel.

Liam: Is there one video I should watch first?

Liam: Wow! The most recent one, about French class, gets right to the point. I'm sorry you had to live through that. 😞 😞

Liam: Too bad I can't add a comment, I certainly would have.

Liam: Something nice, of course!

Liam: I didn't know you weren't a girl or a boy. Cool!

Liam: Hope you don't mind, but you should buy a tripod, sometimes the picture shakes a lot and it's difficult to watch.

Liam: Your brother is cuing you? He looks like you.

Liam: In a good way.

Liam: All right, I'm going to sleep now. See you tomorrow!

He's a good guy. He must have guessed I was away, since I wasn't answering, but he kept on sending messages, lots of them. I wonder why he is so open with me, when he's so mysterious and moody in class. Maybe he was just waiting for someone to make the first move. All I know is, if I were him, I'd be shy about sending a dozen messages without getting an answer. I decide to respond.

Ciel: I'm happy you like the videos. 😄 *Especially with all the trouble they've caused me lately. Sorry I didn't answer before, I go to bed early. Yes, that's my little brother, but appearances are deceiving, he can be a brat. See you soon at school?*

As I finish sending the message, I hear the newspaper truck in front of the house, and the familiar *Bang!* that tells me the delivery guys have thrown my bale of papers on the porch. Off to work!

11

Embarrassed Confusion

After the papers, I take a shower and get dressed as I think about Skyping with Eiríkur this evening. I put on a pretty yellow dress with flowered embroidery, one of my favorites. Wearing the dress makes me think of him. It reminds me of the time I wore it to the anime convention we went to last fall. I feel all nostalgic. Then I wonder if it's not too colorful for school. Too flashy, too young. People will look at me strangely if I wear it. I take it off and put on a black T-shirt, a gray-blue flannel shirt, and jeans.

I contemplate the results in the mirror. I try to fix my messy hair that falls on my shoulders like a hailstorm on a field. Why do Bettie Bobbie and her followers say my hair is ugly? I think it looks pretty cool like this.

I have breakfast with my brother. We hear our father

snoring from his room, and make as little noise as possible. Sometimes he has insomnia and gets real irritable if he doesn't sleep enough.

Just as I'm walking into school, the spring-popping alert on my phone tells me I have a new message. I read it, and my eyes widen.

> *Liam: Hey, my mother told me she met the father of someone who goes to Monet-Chartrand last night at a parents of trans people meeting. Would that be your father by any chance?*

Absorbed in my reading material, I practically crash into Stephie, stacking her notebooks in our locker. She looks my way.

"Good morning, vision of beauty!"

"Stop calling me that, or…"

"Or what?"

"Or I might fall in love with you!"

I blow Stephie a kiss and wink at her.

"No, anything but that!"

Stephie pretends my blown kiss is as powerful as a fist to the face, and she crumples to the floor, moaning. I put my backpack in our locker and take out my math folder. We head for the atrium.

Ciel

"You do anything yesterday?" Stephie asks.

"Not much. I made a new video with Virgil."

"Cool! What about?"

"Bettie Bobbie. But I don't say her name."

"I can smell the drama from here." She sniffs the air as if she were an expert.

"I programed it to be on my channel this afternoon. Oh, something else! I counted up my money, and pretty soon, I should have enough to buy the camera I'm after. Want to come to the store with me?"

Stephie wrinkles up her nose. "I can't tomorrow. My mother and I are going to see a play. But tonight I could."

"I won't have the money until tomorrow. On Thursday I get the tips from my paper route. Anyway, tonight I can't, I'm Skyping with Eiríkur."

"Right, I remember. I bet you can't wait."

Stephie isn't very enthusiastic. I know she still thinks I should drop Eiríkur. I decide to answer casually.

"Sure, I'm looking forward to it, but it's been a little strange lately. I like talking with him, but if it's like the other times, we seem to have fewer and fewer things to say to each other."

"That's normal. How long has it been, six months since he left?"

"Not that long! Just two."

We split up on the third floor, since our classes are in different wings. As Mrs. Campeau, the math teacher, takes attendance, I notice she hesitates a little when she comes to my name, then calls me Alex Sousa, which doesn't really bother me, since this is one of the classes where I was called Alessandro. But by giving me a nickname, it's like Mrs. Campeau and I were best friends forever. The idea makes me laugh. I picture us buying slushies at the corner store on our way to the rec center to watch the kids at the skate park. Annabelle catches me trying not to laugh, and gives me an intrigued look.

I spend the whole class wandering from one thought to the next, from the camera I want to buy, to my date with Eiríkur this evening, to Bettie Bobbie mocking me, to my new friendship with Liam. I think of the look on Zoe's face yesterday at the Gender and Sexuality Alliance meeting, when I told her I have my own YouTube channel. I forgot to send her the link. I wonder how she will react when she learns I'm trans. Will her attitude change?

With my head full of all those thoughts, no wonder I have such bad grades in math!

Toward the end of class, when we are all supposed to be quietly working on an exercise, I feel the need to go to the washroom. I woke up really early, which threw all my body rhythms off-kilter. For example, I'm hungry, which never happens this time of day. I go to see the teacher.

"I finished the exercise. Can I go to the washroom?"

"Now? Class is over in five minutes."

Exactly my point, I feel like telling her. I don't want to have other people in the washroom along with me, and it's always crowded between classes. I could go during my next class, but it's French, and after the embarrassing remarks Madame Walter made the other day, I'd rather not push my luck.

"I'm in a real hurry."

Mrs. Campeau sighs and opens her drawer to take out the hall pass.

"Make it snappy."

She doesn't need to tell me twice. I head for the girls' washroom at top speed. Someone enters while I'm in one of the stalls. Whoever it is dallies in front of the mirror a few seconds, which keeps me from sneaking out. She must be touching up her lipstick or something like that. I don't move a muscle. I wait for her to go.

Finally, she does. I open the door to the stall, wash my hands, and slip out of the washroom. Just then, the bell rings. That's all right, I finished the math exercise. What I don't like is having to fight my way back against the stream of students pouring out of the classrooms to get to their lockers or their next class. Everyone pushes everyone else, no one sees me, and I have all the trouble in the world just to get back to my math class to pick up my things and return the pass to Mrs. Campeau. Before I leave again, she waves me down.

"Can I please have a word with you?"

"Uh, sure."

"We had a teachers' meeting yesterday evening, we were discussing our class lists, and we realized you had told some teachers there was a mistake in the lists. Your name is Alessandra, and not Alessandro, or am I mistaken?"

I feel my face turn red. The blood rushes so fast to my head I'm afraid my nose is going to start bleeding any second now. I was naïve to think I could sail through the year without having to explain to anyone why certain teachers call me Alessandro, and others Alessandra.

"I don't want you to feel uncomfortable," Mrs. Campeau continues. "It doesn't bother me at all if you prefer Alessandra. But just let me know, all right?"

"All right."

"We were also wondering if your parents are aware, in case we have to contact them."

"Aware of what?"

"That you prefer being a girl."

"I don't prefer being a girl. Or a boy, for that matter."

Mrs. Campeau looks more confused than ever.

136

"You can act like I'm a girl, if it's less complicated for you," I add. "And my father is aware, thanks for asking."

"Oh, fine," Mrs. Campeau says. "For your information, he can have your name changed on the attendance lists with a note from a psychologist, but for the report cards, he needs to contact the Ministry of Education."

"I'll tell him."

"Do you want me to tell the other teachers to call you Alessandra?"

I think it over a moment.

"Yes, please. But say it might change again, because life is full of uncertainty."

♥ ♥ ♥

I figure I did pretty well with Mrs. Campeau. On the way to French, I replay the conversation in my head. As for her suggestion, I'm not sure it's worth the trouble going to see a psychologist to have my name changed.

When my mother died, I had to see a psychologist for a few months, because I stopped talking to people, and I was feeling more and more depressed.

It didn't work out very well. Even if I wasn't seeing the psychologist for that, she kept going on about my role in the family, how I was the "big brother," and had to "show the way by being strong"—stuff like that.

I remember she took it upon herself to tell me that I "walked like a girl," and that I should change to "appear more confident." She really made me feel like less than nothing. As you can imagine, the idea of seeing another psychologist doesn't exactly appeal to me.

I get to French two minutes before class begins. Madame Walter says, "*Bonjour,*" and I answer. At our table, where Stephie and I usually sit, at the front of the class, I see another student. I'm surprised. No one has changed places since the beginning of the year. Who does he think he is? I take a quick look around and see Stephie wearing the red jacket she had on this morning, talking to two girls I don't recognize. Since I hadn't shown up, she must have sat with them, and that's how we lost our spot.

She catches my eye and shrugs her shoulders, disappointed. There isn't another free two-person table in the room. I'll have to sit with someone I don't know. I sigh, unsure what to do, then scan the room again. That's when I spot Liam, sitting alone at his usual table, lost in his thoughts. I gather up my courage.

"Can I sit here?"

When he sees me, his eyes light up and he smiles.

"Of course! Here."

He takes his bag off the back of the free chair, and I sit down.

"Someone stole my spot in front."

"Better call the cops," he says with a smile. "Actually, it works out, because I need to talk to you. My mother told me to ask you if you wanted to have lunch at our place today. She met your father at the meeting last night, and really liked him."

"That's nice, but I have my lunch."

"You can eat it at our house. We're right next door."

I look at Stephie across the room, chatting with her new girlfriends. I know she likes me to eat with her, but I don't think she'd mind if I missed lunch once. It's not like we do a lot of talking when we're surrounded by everyone else.

"What do you say?" Liam asks.

"Sure, glad to."

"Cool! I told you about my cat, right? You're not allergic, I hope."

"Not at all."

I'm excited about going to Liam's, and I can hardly concentrate on what Madame Walter is telling us.

When the bell rings, I ask Liam to wait. I run over to Stephie and alert her that I won't be eating with her today. She gives me a little play slap.

"No fair, I'm jealous! I want to live near school too. See you at the locker, after school?"

"For sure!"

I go back to Liam, who is slipping on a green windbreaker. It floats around him like a flag, despite the sweatshirt he is wearing underneath, which is also three times too big for him. I pick up my books, then we go down the stairs to get my lunchbox from my locker.

"Ooh! Your little crocodile is so cute!" Liam exclaims when I open the door.

"That's Georgette, our locker mascot."

Liam gives Georgette a friendly tap on the snout, which sends her spinning. I watch him from the corner of my eye. I like his calm and collected attitude, as if he were in his living room, wearing a pair of bunny slippers, and not in this giant school. He has this way of saying "Ooh," trying to look serious, but without hiding his feelings.

As we head for his house, Liam tells me about his mother. He lives alone with her. She is a painter and has just started teaching painting in an art school a few mornings a week. He has a big sister named Oceane who lives in an apartment on the Plateau with her boyfriend, Youssef. His father lives in the Gaspé. He only sees him two weeks a year, during the summer.

"It's funny, for me it's the opposite. I live with my father and my little brother. There's my uncle Guilherme, my father's brother, who's here in Montreal, but otherwise, the rest of my father's family is in Brazil."

"Have you been there?"

"Yes, a couple times, when I was three and six. Before I transitioned. I don't know how that part of the family would react if they saw me now, but my grandmother always calls me Ciel when we talk on the phone. She knows I like the name."

"That's because it's cute! What about your mother's side?"

"I don't know, I haven't seen them since she died. I'm WhatsApp friends with two of my aunts, but that's all."

Liam stops and looks at me sadly. "I'm sorry about that."

"It's all right now. It's been a while. I remember not liking my grandfather. When we were together, he'd make all kinds of remarks about how I dressed, how I walked, how I talked. He thought I was too effeminate."

"If he knew you're a girl!"

I correct Liam right away.

"I'm not exactly a girl."

"Excuse me. I should know, I watched all your videos yesterday. I've rarely heard of people who are neither girls nor boys. Uh, when you were born, you were…"

"A baby!"

Liam laughs softly, and his arm brushes mine.

"Now, that's a surprise. What I mean is…"

"My parents and the doctors thought I was a boy."

"I see. Sorry, I just wanted to be sure. They thought I was a girl."

"When did you transition?"

"I must have been five or six. I don't really remember."

"That's young!"

"I was lucky. My mother's best friend is trans, so she understood right away. And since I wasn't going to school, I never had the usual problems."

Liam points to an apartment with an accessibility ramp covering the two steps that lead up to the door.

"Here's my place."

"It's nice! You said you didn't go to school. What do you mean?"

"I was home-schooled until last year."

Suddenly, I understand his strange behavior in class. Now I know why he looks so lost and alone at school, even if he is very friendly.

He opens the door and invites me in. The apartment is big and bright and, most of all, very colorful. The walls are covered with paintings (done by his mother?) and drawings (I bet Liam is the artist behind that one!), along with photographs and mosaics.

We go into the living room, where piles of books are everywhere. The room is messy, but alive. The opposite of my place. The cat with the funny name, Eugene

Leroux, meows as we come in. He is posted by a window covered with stained glass. I get why there's a cat box odor, mixed with incense. An odd smell, in any case.

"Mom, we're home!"

Liam's mother's voice calls back from another room. "Be right there! I'm washing my hands."

Liam asks me to take off my shoes, then gives me the guided tour of the apartment. He shows me the living room (we're already there), his room (he opens the door quickly, revealing mountains of clothes on the floor, then closes it just as fast), the bathroom (practical), his mother's room (he doesn't open the door), and guides me toward the kitchen.

As we go down the hallway, I notice some black-and-white photographs on the wall. They look very old. On one, I see two children in dresses, with long hair. Strange, but I recognize Liam's face. My father once showed me the same type of family photos, but they dated from the 1950s. Unless Liam can travel through time, it couldn't be him in those pictures.

"Who are those people?"

"My sister and I. My mother is in that one."

"Long hair doesn't really suit you," I tease him.

Liam pretends to be offended. "Don't say that! I had long hair up until this summer. And everybody said I looked good."

"Why do those photos have that old-fashioned look?"

"My mother had a phase when she was interested in traditional photography. She had her own darkroom to develop the pictures, back in our last apartment."

"That's a weird thing to get interested in," I say.

"You're the one who's weird!"

I elbow him in the ribs, and he laughs.

The kitchen is as spacious and colorful as the living room. I hear water running in a room next door, which seems one level lower. A curtain serves as a door, and a wooden handrail leads down toward the room.

"That's my mother's studio," Liam tells me. "It was a garage before we moved here, but we don't have a car. You want to see?"

"Sure."

I look around the studio. It's obvious the space is dedicated to art. There are paintings hung everywhere, shelves loaded down with paint pots and brushes, rolls of canvas, a wide table, easels, and more. In the middle of this whirlwind of color is Liam's mother, her back to us. She swivels her wheelchair in our direction after wiping her hands.

"Hello, hello! We don't often have visitors. Sorry for the mess. What's your name again? I forgot."

"Alessandra. Actually, it's Ciel."

"Ciel is their artist's name," Liam explains. "They make YouTube videos. They're really good!"

"Is that so? Your father didn't say anything about that. And he spent all evening yesterday talking about you. It seems you're very intelligent."

Now that's music to my ears. My father really said that? Talk about a surprise! My grades are always just average, or below, at report-card time. It warms my heart to know he thinks that way. Usually he says I'm funny, pretty, and creative, which isn't a bad start.

Liam's mother offers her hand, and I shake it, shyly.

"I'm Sylvie, pleased to meet you! I didn't prepare anything, I've been working all morning."

"It's okay, Mom, they have their lunch. And I'll make myself a sandwich."

"Good idea. I'm due for a break, anyway."

We go into the kitchen. Sylvie moves toward the counter to tidy up.

"Can I help?" I ask.

"How nice of you! No, just make yourself at home, start eating. I know they don't give you much time at school."

"That's for sure," Liam agrees, taking some items out of the fridge. "Should I make you a sandwich, Mom?"

"No, thanks. You always add too much mayonnaise." His mother smiles. "In any case, Alessandra, your father was talking a mile a minute yesterday, at the parents' meeting. He was very sincere, though a little awkward."

"Awkward?"

"Yes. He doesn't know the subject very well, and he has a hard time finding the right words. But he loves you, and it's obvious he wants to learn."

I don't know what to think as I listen to Sylvie. My father doesn't know the subject? I wouldn't say that. He has read every book in the world about trans people.

I open my lunchbox and start eating, and Liam joins me at the table with his sandwich. His mother finishes cleaning the counter and comes over to us, talking the whole time.

"I must say, a few new fathers are a welcome sight at the meeting. I try to go as often as possible, and most of the time, only mothers are there. But yesterday, Martin wasn't the only man. There was another one who had been there before, but I forgot his name. A Brazilian."

Just as I suspected. Sylvie isn't talking about my father, but Stephie's. She was supposed to be invited for lunch, not me! All of a sudden, I feel sad. And embarrassed too. I don't know how to react. Sylvie notices.

"Are you all right, Alessandra?" she asks kindly.

"Yes. But there's one thing…"

Think fast, I tell myself. I don't want to lie to Sylvie, but I can't let on that Stephie is trans. She works so hard so the fewest people possible will find out. I feel like I'm hurting her cause by hanging out with her, and I don't want to make the situation worse. Summoning my courage, I answer.

"My father's name isn't Martin," I say.

A brief moment of silence, then Liam slaps himself on the forehead as if he can't believe what's happening. His mother laughs nervously.

"Oops, I'm sorry, Alessandra," she says. "Luckily I didn't talk very much about the personal things Martin told me."

"Mom, really," Liam says, rolling his eyes.

"But he did say his daughter is in first year at Monet-Chartrand," Sylvie adds.

"That's why my mother talked about it, and why I was sure it was you," Liam explains.

"It's true, when I think about it, you look much more like the other man who was there. What's your father's name again?"

I get that sinking feeling. I don't like to be compared to my father, not physically, even if I know that people have good intentions when they point out the resemblance. But I always feel they are remarking on the "masculine" traits I inherited from him, as if they were secretly suggesting that I look like a man.

"Gabriel Lucas Sousa," I answer, trying to hide my discomfort.

"That's it, that's him! Sorry for the confusion."

"That means there's another trans person in our classes," Liam deduces. "Who could that be?"

"An absolute mystery," I say, concentrating hard on my lunch.

Liam turns to his mother. "You were saying her father was awkward and not very comfortable with the subject. Maybe his daughter has transitioned at home only and is still living as a boy at school. What do you think, Ciel?"

I shrug my shoulders. No comment. Finally, Sylvie changes the subject, and very discreetly, I let out a sigh of relief.

Saved by the bell!

12

The Importance of Great White Sharks

The afternoon goes by fast. During the break, I take a few minutes to authorize the publication of the new video I programmed earlier from my phone. With some apprehension, I see it is now available on my channel. What impact will it have? I wonder.

At the end of the day, I meet Stephie at our locker.

"Ready for your romantic encounter?" she asks with a wink.

She means my Skype call with Eiríkur at four. I smile.

"Don't exaggerate. It's not like we're still going out together, or anything like that. There's nothing exciting."

"Right. Eiríkur doesn't seem too excited to talk to you."

"You don't understand! It took us only four days to organize the call. That's a record for him."

"How many messages has he sent since he went back to Iceland?"

I start counting in my head. Nine, ten, eleven? Maybe eleven. Eleven emails in just under two months? But I'm not sure, and I decide I don't really want to know.

"That doesn't mean anything," I say, defending my boyfriend. "Just because we're a different kind of couple from you and Frank doesn't mean it can't work."

"I never said we were perfect," Stephie answers, leaning on the next locker. "But I'm sad that you're spending all your time counting the days before he finally remembers to tear his attention away from his video games and think of you. Promise me you'll ask him to do a little better when you talk to him."

"I don't want to push too hard. He has his life, I have mine. That's all."

Stephie sighs. I'm clinging to Eiríkur, and she's disappointed.

"Okay. Will you call me afterward?"

"Why? You want to have a romantic encounter with me too?"

She bursts out laughing.

"I hereby inform you," I say in a fake haughty voice, "that if you wish to speak to me, you must set a meeting by email at least four days in advance."

As we move toward the exit, she takes my arm and whispers into my ear.

"That doesn't apply to me. I have best-friend privileges."

♥ ♥ ♥

My father is sitting on the sofa when I come in. He's working on his laptop, surrounded by papers covered with scribbles, most likely assignments he's correcting. When he sees me, he takes off his glasses and rubs his eyes.

"Hey there, sprout! You look like you're in a good mood. Did you do a good deed at school?"

"I sat with a boy who's always by himself in French. But only because someone had taken the table where Stephie and I always sit, but still, I'm happy I did it, and then he invited me to eat lunch at his place."

"Really? What's his name?"

My father pushes aside the papers cluttering the sofa so I can sit down. I like to sit on the armrest, even if he doesn't want me to.

"Liam. And you know what? His mother was at the meeting for parents of trans kids yesterday, and Stephie's father talked to her a whole lot. He told her his daughter goes to Monet-Chartrand. Then she told Liam about it, and since he knows I'm trans, he thought I was Martin's child."

"That's a coincidence. Do you remember his mother's name?"

"Not really. No."

"Somehow, I'm not surprised." My father laughs, tousling my hair.

"Why? Because I have the memory of a goldfish? Let's see, she's a painter, and she's in a wheelchair."

"That's Sylvie! I've met her a few times at the parents' meetings. She's very nice. Yesterday, Martin didn't need me at all; she spent the evening talking with him. I thought her son was being home-schooled."

"Not anymore, it seems. I don't know why."

From the top of the armrest, I swing my feet, trying to remember what I wanted to talk to my father about. Right—the camera! I almost forgot.

"Dad, remember the camera I want to buy for my videos? It's on sale at Galeries d'Anjou. I did the math, and if I get enough tips tomorrow when I deliver the paper, I'll be able to buy it tomorrow evening."

"How much is it?"

"Five hundred and ten dollars, tax and tripod included."

"That's a pile of money!"

"Sure, but it's a lot less expensive than normal. It's a super discount. I don't want to miss the sale. And, then, I wanted to ask…. If I don't make enough tips tomorrow, would you mind lending me twenty dollars?"

My father smiles. "I'd be glad to, my young businessperson—I mean, artist."

"Oh, thank you!"

I'd like to throw my arms around him, but I'm afraid of ruining the fragile balance of the stacks of assignments on the sofa. Instead, I give him my brightest smile. He looks pensive.

"Are you going to keep your paper route after you buy the camera?"

"I don't think so."

"Reconsider it. Normally you have to give two weeks' notice to your employer, so they have the time to find a replacement. You should call Mrs. Barbeau as soon as possible and tell her."

Mrs. Barbeau is the paper's delivery coordinator. She has a way of intimidating me. I'm always afraid of not sounding "professional" enough when I talk to her, even if she always tells me that I'm doing a good job. I don't feel like calling her, but I guess I don't have the choice.

"Later, okay? I have a Skype date with Eiríkur in a few minutes."

"Oh, really? You can take care of it afterward. Do you want me to go work in the kitchen? You'll have more privacy."

"Yes, please."

My father gathers up his mess and carries it to the kitchen table. I sit down in front of the computer and make sure the microphone is connected and that Skype is functioning. Seven endless minutes separate me from four o'clock. I take a look at YouTube. The video I uploaded this afternoon has been viewed several times, thanks to my new subscribers, but so far, the results aren't extraordinary. I hope Bettie Bobbie will watch it and understand I'm talking about her.

I get a message on Skype.

Eiríkur: I'm here. Ready?

My heart starts beating hard.

Ciel: Yes!

I click to begin the video call. The alert rings a few seconds later, then Eiríkur's handsome round face appears on my screen. I'm so happy to see him.

I go first.

"Hi there!"

He answers with his thick Scandinavian accent. "Hello. How are things?"

"Fine. Much better when I see your face."

"You're cute, you know that?"

"And you're funny. It must be night in Iceland."

"Yes. But two weeks ago, it was still daylight."

"Wow! Hey, guess what? I'm finally going to be able to buy my video camera—tomorrow!"

"Good for you. You've been talking about it forever."

"You'll see, the videos I'm going to make will be spec-tac-u-lar."

"I can't wait."

Silence settles in. I smile. He smiles back shyly. Showing affection has never been his strong point. Then I say what I promised I would.

"I'm happy to see you. It's been a while. These last few weeks have been hard for me. We haven't written much."

"Yes, I know. It's my fault, and I'm sorry."

"You're busy, I understand."

"No, that's not the problem. Ciel…I just wanted to say I miss you. Really. I wish I were in Montreal to watch movies and play video games with you. I think you're great."

His words do me so much good. A great weight has been lifted from my shoulders. I feel tears come to my eyes.

"You're so sweet. I miss you a lot too."

"I'm sorry I took so much time answering your last emails. I couldn't find the right words. That's why I wanted us to call this week. I wanted to tell you that I love you very much."

"Me too."

"But a long-distance relationship is too hard for me."

I stop breathing. I know what's going to happen next, and I don't want to go through it. Slowly, Eiríkur says what he has to say.

"When I think of you, it's just too painful. You and I are so far apart. And I know my parents will never go back to live in Montreal. Not any time soon."

In a weak voice, I ask, "Do you want to split up?"

Eiríkur looks so sad. It breaks my heart a second time to see him unhappy.

"It's not because I don't love you anymore. I think you're special. Honestly."

I can't hold them back. Tears run down my face. My mind is in a fog. I don't understand what I'm feeling.

"You are too. The same," I manage to say.

"I think it would be better if we were just friends."

He is having trouble speaking too. I see that he's crying. Time goes by, and neither of us says a word. We both dry our tears. I wipe my face on my sleeve. My head is spinning, and I feel dizzy.

Then I catch my breath and tell him, very softly, "We had some good times together, right?"

Eiríkur tries to smile.

"Right. Remember that time we put up posters all over the city? We wrote 'Lost Cat' on them, but it was just a photo of your hand with cat ears and whiskers drawn on it?"

I can't help smiling when I think of that day.

"I remember. A policeman stopped and told us not to put posters on the traffic lights. Good thing he didn't see it was a just a joke."

"And then you told him in a very sad voice, 'But, sir, we're looking for my cat!'"

"He softened up and wished us good luck!"

I laugh so hard through my tears that I nearly suffocate.

"Yeah, that was funny."

We smile.

"Do you want to go on writing?" I ask.

"I'd like that, if you want to."

Eiríkur and I talk for another half hour at least. We laugh a lot, and we cry a lot too. It hurts that we won't be together anymore, but when we finally say good-bye, I tell myself that Stephie was right. The relationship was complicated, and it made me anxious. I just hope she won't say "I told you so!" when I give her the news, and then put on a compassionate look and call me her "poor little darling." I sit in front of the computer, and don't move, and try to understand what just happened.

My little brother was out walking Borki, and now he comes into the apartment. He calls as he goes through the living room, then stops suddenly in the hall in front of his room.

"You okay?"

I nod my head. He shrugs his shoulders, then disappears.

Like a robot, I stand and walk to my bed, then collapse onto it. The blanket is cool against my burning cheeks. I feel very alone. I don't know why, but I think of my mother, the warmth of her arms. I wish I could curl up next to her.

I grab my phone and send Stephie a message:

> *It's over with Eiríkur.*

A minute or two later, I get her answer:

Poor darling

Are you all right?

Want me to come over?

I think about it. It's nice of her to offer. But is that really what I need right now? Then why did I text her? Certainly because I need comforting. And that means in person.

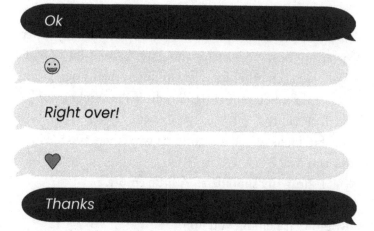

Ok

Right over!

Thanks

No worries. On my way.

Stephie is coming to support me in this difficult time. That consoles me and gives me strength. I feel completely dehydrated after crying so much. I get a big glass of water in the kitchen, and there is my father, buried under piles of papers, with more scattered across the table. He looks up.

"How did your date go?"

"I don't know. All right, I guess. But Eiríkur and I aren't together anymore."

I thought I had calmed down, but my throat tightens up when I say the words, and I'm afraid I'm going to start crying again.

"Oh, love, I'm so sorry."

He stands up and throws his arms around me. With the glass of water in one hand, I hold him with my other arm, my head against his shoulder. I feel a lot lighter. We hold each other for a few minutes, then I step away.

"I texted Stephie. Is it all right if she comes over?"

"Of course!"

He looks at me a second or two, then asks, "How do you feel?"

I shrug my shoulders. "A little empty."

"If I told you we were having lasagna for dinner, would that help fill you up?"

I answer him with a hug. I spill some water on his shirt, but he doesn't mind. He kisses the top of my head.

"Tonight, you should do only things you like, okay? It's normal to be sad. Eiríkur means a lot to you, after all the time you spent together. It's good to let your sadness out, but also realize that you have the right to be happy. Think of a thing you'd like to do."

I think about it. Not so much the question he wants me to ask myself, but the way he makes me feel good. He knows how to help me understand my emotions, instead of telling me what they should be.

"I'm not sure. It's nice out, I could go to the park with Stephie."

My father takes out his wallet and hands me a twenty-dollar bill.

"Make one last visit to the ice-cream stand on Beaubien, before it closes for the season. Invite Stephie. I'm paying."

I thank him and take the money. I'm not a big fan of ice cream, unlike Stephie, who loves it. Getting out interests me more than ice cream.

"You can go after dinner. It'll be ready soon. Has Stephie eaten?"

"I don't know. I'll ask her if she wants to have dinner with us."

I go out and wait for her on the steps of the back

porch. I'm barefoot, even if it's a little chilly. But none of that matters anymore.

A few minutes later, I see her opening the gate that leads into the yard. She locks her bike at the foot of the stairway, beneath me. She looks up and smiles. Then climbs the stairs and sits down.

"What did he say?"

I sigh. It's painful to think of everything that happened.

"He said he still loves me, but a long-distance relationship doesn't work for him."

"Oh, Ciel darling," Stephie tells me with a sad look.

"Honestly, I don't know if it would have worked for me in the long run."

"It didn't seem very easy."

"If he was online as often as I am, maybe we could have continued. But the time difference complicated things."

Stephie listens quietly, letting me talk, watching the trees in the yard wave their branches in the wind. I give her a gentle poke in the ribs.

"I forgot to mention it, but do you want to eat dinner here? My father made lasagna."

Stephie ends up staying for dinner. She even gets involved in a long conversation with my father, which is perfect for me, since I don't feel like talking. Virgil tries to impress her by displaying his knowledge of great white sharks and boasting about his scores in the latest *Zelda* game. I told you Stephie was good with kids. That includes my nine-year-old brother. She gives him so much quality attention when she comes over that he has raised her to the status of goddess and begun worshiping her. You should see his reaction when she opens her eyes wide and says "Wow!" and "Really? You're good!" to make him feel better.

After dinner, she and I go to the ice-cream stand, near the city swimming pool. The pool has been closed since Labor Day, but the stand usually stays open into October. It's strange to be going this time of year, when the leaves are starting to turn red, and it's cool enough in the evening to wear a sweater. I don't feel much like eating ice cream, but I'm happy for the chance to go walking with my friend. She helps me get some fresh air into my thoughts.

The sunset is spectacular. With the cloudy day we had, I figured the sky would be gray, and that we wouldn't see anything, but the wind has swept away the clouds, and suddenly, everything is pink and fiery orange. It doesn't take long to get to the ice-cream place.

A good thing, because Stephie has just about used up all her usual subjects of conversation: her parents getting on her nerves, our school's dress code that's too strict ("All skirts must be down to the knees"—can you believe it?), Frank's last soccer game, and the new color she wants to paint her room at her mother's. At the stand, we run into a flock of kids, twenty or more, who have just finished playing a soccer game. Stephie and I are afraid they'll hold us up, but their coach has already put in their order. We get our desserts a few minutes later. A caramel milkshake for her, and soft ice cream with pieces of cheesecake in it for me.

With mini-soccer players pushing and shoving, we decide to stroll in Louisiana Park. After the baseball field, there are little hills, more like bumps, still lit by the sun, though it's quickly sinking behind the buildings. We sit down.

Stephie lies on the grass. She pats her stomach, her invitation for me to lay my head there. Gladly. My head gently rises and falls as she breathes in and out. She is an excellent pillow for me to eat my ice cream on.

A few minutes go by in silence. She drinks her milkshake and watches me think about Eiríkur. It must be obvious. I look lost and sad. Even if I haven't said his name in at least twenty minutes.

"I wonder if it's true, that we'll go on writing to each other," I think out loud.

Stephie doesn't answer. Usually she's good at cheering me up, but she rarely says things she doesn't believe just to make me feel better. She puts down her milkshake, which is almost finished, and starts stroking my hair as I watch the clouds come together and break apart for a setting sun that doesn't seem impressed.

13

Raccoons and Rainbow Cookies

I spent a sleepless night. Not only because of the nightmares—the slightest sound would wake me up. The cars on the boulevard, someone laughing in the street, my brother stubbing his toe on the way to the bathroom, Borki lapping at his water, the upstairs neighbors taking a shower…. I would awake with a start and check the alarm clock, trying to calculate how many minutes I had before 5:45.

I hope my special power that wakes me up two minutes before the alarm won't disappear. That would be tragic! I read somewhere that a person can lose certain abilities after suffering a trauma. I wonder if my breakup with Eiríkur counts as a trauma.

Yesterday evening, after Stephie left, my father helped me find Mrs. Barbeau's phone number, and I called her to say I was quitting. To my surprise, she was happy, since she was just about to contact me to announce that the paper is going online. In a month, the print version will disappear, and subscribers will have to read it on the Internet. All the paper routes will be canceled.

I'm a little sad to leave my job, but once I buy my video camera, I won't need to work. Finally, I'll be able to sleep a little longer in the morning.

But this morning, I wake up early, prepare the newspapers, and put them in my bag, making sure to throw the plastic ties in the garbage, the way my father wants me to. This will be one of the last times I'll go out on my bike so early. That's a little strange. But not as strange as not having a boyfriend anymore.

One thing bothers me. All the time we were together, Eiríkur and I hardly ever kissed. I would have liked to more often. But he didn't like the idea of someone else's saliva in his mouth. If I ever have someone new in my life, I'll make sure that doesn't bother them.

As I step outside, I remember that today is tip day. Along my route, my pocket fills with one- and two-dollar coins, and five-dollar bills. I imagine paying for the camera with change. I'm sure the cashier will find that hilarious—or maybe not.

I'm closing in on Dr. Mahelona's house, the man

who gives me a generous tip when he gets the paper early, the way he likes it. The suspense grows, since I need to make as much as I usually do if I want to buy the tripod at the same time as the camera. My father agreed to help out, but I would rather have the complete amount myself.

I get off my bike and go up the asphalt walkway, past the lawn that seems to have been abandoned for the autumn. I zero in on the porch. As always, I make as little noise as possible to keep the raccoons from knowing I'm there. Who knows what they might do? They could scratch out your eyes or put a curse on your first-born child if you scare them.

I climb the three wooden steps carefully. The coast is clear. I open the cover of the metal mailbox. Inside is the plastic case. A bill is waiting there, and I slip it out of the case and hold it up so the streetlight can reveal the amount. Twenty dollars! I jump for joy, and all on their own, my feet do the shuffle-step, shuffle-toe that I learned in tap dance class last year. The whole porch vibrates. The lids of the garbage can, the recycling, the compost, and the vermicompost pop open all at the same time, as if to celebrate my success, but then four raccoons leap into the air like evil spirits from a horror movie, crying and squealing and yowling so I leave the premises in a hurry. No need to ask twice. I rush back to my bike, then remember. In the heat of the moment, I forgot to leave the doctor's paper in his mailbox.

I roll it tightly and slip a rubber band around it, then throw it onto the porch, hoping the raccoons won't chew it to pieces. They eat everything else, so why not?

Slumped back in my chair, I count the minutes until the lunch bell rings. Time is standing still, I'm so tired. And then there's this: I brought the money to buy the camera to school, so I can go directly to the store after class. I put the money in a plastic bag, and zipped it into the front pocket of my backpack. But still, I'm feeling paranoid. What if someone steals my money? It's the beginning of the year, and already a boy in my math class had his protractor stolen. This place is a real jungle. Under my desk, I clench my knees nervously around my bag.

In both classes this morning, the teachers called me Alessandra instead of Alessandro when they took attendance. Mrs. Campeau must have told them to do that after our little talk yesterday. My name didn't make any waves in English, but in ethics and world views, some kids thought it was funny, or strange. There were a few murmurs, but nothing more.

The bell frees me, and I go to wait for Stephie at our locker. This morning we agreed to meet to continue yesterday's philosophical discussion about why some boys have this constant need to prove their virility to themselves. But knowing her, as soon as we hit the cafeteria, she'll start talking with her new girlfriends and forget about me.

"I see you're surviving your day," she says when she shows up.

"So far. My ethics and world views teacher spent the period telling us about his vacation in southern France. I nearly drifted off to sleep."

"Lucky duck!" Stephie answers with her ironic smile. "I just had math. The teacher talked the whole time about his baby. Does he really think we care? I was close enough to see the photo he was showing, though. Maybe he's right, the baby is pretty cute."

"You have Liam Johnson in math, don't you?"

"Yes, why? Do you want me to tell him you're available now? You move fast!"

"Come on, don't say that. I want to ask him if he feels like going to the camera store this afternoon."

"That's not fair, I wanted to go!"

"Then you should have been available. That'll teach you to go on all kinds of exciting adventures with your mother."

"I don't think we can call a trip to the theater an exciting adventure. If you wait until tomorrow, I'll go."

"I'm feeling too depressed after what happened with Eiríkur. The camera will be my breakup present to myself."

Stephie puts on an outraged face, which I know is just an act. "And you want to buy it with a guy you just met instead of waiting for your best friend? I can't believe it. Not that I'm judging you, and for sure, Liam is pretty handsome…."

"You said it—wait, that has nothing to do with it!"

"Like I believe you. Can't you send him a message?"

"He doesn't have a phone."

"No way! How does he talk to his friends?"

"He produces sounds with his vocal cords, like this: *blecchh!*"

We laugh as we head for our table and Stephie's friends. When I come into the cafeteria, all eyes turn in my direction, and I wonder if there's something written in capital letters on my forehead, because why else would I attract so much attention? Annabelle, the one who wore glasses last year, but who has switched to contact lenses, stands up.

"Can I give you a hug?"

I don't know what to say. Stephie, Eiríkur, my

brother, my father, and Borki are the only ones who have given me a hug over the last year.

"Uh, I guess so."

She holds me very tight in her arms. "I went through a breakup last June," she says in a broken voice, "and it wasn't easy. I'm here for you if you want to talk."

"Thanks."

I sit down at the table. A large plastic platter is sitting in the center like a throne.

Felicia, the one with the Afro, says to me softly, "When I heard what happened yesterday, I sent you a message on WhatsApp."

"Sorry. I went to bed early."

"That's what I figured. Since we couldn't talk, I decided to make you cookies."

She lifts the cover off the platter, and shows me a couple dozen Smarties cookies. Proud of herself, she tells me, "Rainbow cookies for the one who brightens up our day! They're a present for you, but I think there are enough for everybody, if you feel like sharing."

I blush. I never expected so much sympathy from people whose names I hardly know—even if I see them every day.

"Thanks, but you shouldn't have taken the trouble."

"Come on! You're one of the nicest people in this school. You don't deserve to be sad."

I glance at Stephie. She's watching me with a kind look. Obviously, she told the girls that I was going through a hard time. It's good to know I can trust them. I feel silly about doubting their sincerity, and whether they really wanted to be my friends. Maybe, after all, not everybody thinks bad things about me.

Then I start to cry, right in front of the platter of cookies. I'm mad at myself. I shouldn't have been afraid to talk to them.

"If you like, since I live right next door, we can drop off our stuff and then go to the shopping center," Liam tells me.

"Fine with me."

I'm sitting with Liam in French, the last class of the day. That was Stephie's idea, since I wanted to talk with him, and she felt like being with another friend. But we promised, next time, we would sit together for good.

The bell rings, and we head for Liam's place. We stop to say hello to his mother, busily painting in her garage studio, then go up to Liam's room, which is a painful mess, to drop off our packs. I carefully transfer the money into a small bag I wear over my shoulder.

I gaze at the mountains of clothes heaped on top of the furniture. On a cork board, I see the article about him, along with some realistic drawings of machines and robots. I move closer for a better look.

"Did you draw these?"

He looks uncomfortable. He must not like to talk about his skills, artistic or athletic.

"I did, but I didn't invent them. I copied them from mangas, or off the TV."

"You can really draw!"

We don't stay in his room for long, just long enough for me to notice, between two piles of clean clothes on the dresser, some home-made motorized creatures, and vehicles made of Lego that look quite complex. Liam would get along great with my brother. But then again, everyone gets along with Liam.

We exit his room, and Liam calls to his mother that we're leaving, and she answers, her mind clearly elsewhere. We hurry to catch the bus and spend most of the trip in silence. I decide to mention that my boyfriend broke up with me yesterday.

"Didn't you talk about him in a video? I'm sorry to hear that."

"I'll be all right. Last night was pretty painful, but after all, we haven't seen each other for over two months."

"Things must be hard. You were together a while, weren't you?"

"Almost a year."

"That's a lot. The longest I was with someone was three weeks. And we didn't even kiss."

"We didn't kiss much either, Eiríkur and I. It didn't interest him. It's not something that interests me much either now. I'm not very intimate with people."

A moment later, I tell him, "I feel like I'll never fall in love. Sometimes I envy Stephie, my best girlfriend."

"The one you sit with in French?"

"That's her. She falls in love with the first boy who looks her way. And girls interest her too, sometimes. She has a boyfriend, but that doesn't keep her from falling for other people. But it never lasts long, because Frank and her, it's like love with a capital L. They've been going out for nearly two years."

"Really? Wow! Frank's the Lebanese guy who always wears tracksuits?"

"Aha, you noticed him?"

"We have math and social studies together, so I see him pretty often. I thought of making a list of all the Impact players' shirts he has. I bet he wears a different one every day."

"Do you ever talk to him?"

"No, why?"

"No reason," I say, pulling at the seam of my jeans. "I'm just surprised you remember his name. There are so many people in our classes! And you don't know anyone from the year before, because you weren't even in school."

"You probably won't believe me, but I have this special power. I remember the names of everyone I meet. When the teachers take attendance in class, I play a little game with myself. I try to pick out the person the teacher is calling before they answer."

Is he serious? I can't believe he and I could be so different.

"Oh, I believe you," I tell him. "I have a special power too, but it's not nearly as practical as yours. You'll laugh if I tell you."

"I want to know!"

"In the morning, I always wake up two minutes before the alarm clock goes off. No matter what time it is."

"Now, that's really useful. Usually I wake up an hour or two *after* it rings!"

I smile to myself. Maybe, deep down, he and I are complementary. And maybe it's more interesting that way.

♥ ♥ ♥

The clerk in the photography department takes the camera out of the display case, and finally I am holding it, after all the effort I made to get to this point. Tears of joy come to my eyes. My face flushes with excitement, but I don't mind. I'm happy, and my head is filled with future projects.

The cashier does not appreciate my paying half the amount with my debit card, and the rest in bills and coins. It takes her forever to count it all. Finally, she hands me my receipt, and I can leave with my video camera and tripod, and a light heart.

"You sure you don't want me to carry the bag?" Liam offers. "It looks heavy."

"You can take the tripod, but no way anyone is going to touch my precious baby!"

"If you say so! Now that you have the camera, what are you going to do?"

"Make better videos—what else!"

Liam laughs. "Of course. But what's the point of making better videos? Do you want to be a professional YouTuber? Make TV programs? Be an actor?"

I think it over. I had never considered the question.

"Actually, I don't know. Right now, I just want to make videos. I heard that if you have enough subscribers and a lot of people watch your videos, YouTube pays you money. At least, that's what I read."

"That would be cool! It could be your job. Hey, since we're here, do you mind going to Cruella, next to Simon's? The last time I was there, they had a cap I liked, but I didn't have the money."

"You came all this way for me, it's the least I can do. I know the store, I go there with my best friend sometimes."

Stephie doesn't know what she's missing. I'm sure, right now, she must be finishing dinner, and about to enjoy an unforgettable evening at the theater with her mother—unless they went to a restaurant first, spoiled child that she is! Compared to that, hanging out at the mall with me must seem pretty boring. But I can't help it—I feel like I'm cheating on her by going to Cruella with someone else.

The store has a lot of good stuff, but the atmosphere is morose. That's their trademark. Past the shelves loaded with black and white and red clothes, there are all kinds of decorations: plastic gargoyles, stuffed cats that manage to be both adorable and frightening, posters of little girls with empty eyes.

I like the place for the clothes. Lots of lace and original styles. I bought my favorite shirt here, with rows of lace on the front and a Peter Pan collar.

"I would take everything they have on the shelves," I tell Liam. "Even in the men's section, they have sweaters I like. Too bad they're so expensive."

"It's a store for the rich. But I'm lucky, my father transferred me some money this week to buy clothes. Sometimes he does that, like he thinks that will make me love him. But I haven't seen him since the end of last school year."

"How can that be?"

"He lives in the Gaspé, remember? It's a ten-hour drive from here."

"Don't you ever visit him?"

"I went last year, and it was really boring. He has an apartment in Percé, but since he works at a mine three or four days a week, up in the mountains, he's not there very much. There's nothing to do. A big TV takes up the whole wall, but it doesn't get any channels."

As he tells me about his father, we stroll through the store, looking for the cap he wants. I want to stop and examine every item. The clothes are so original, and they look great.

"I'm surprised you like Cruella," I tell Liam. "It doesn't seem like your style."

"I like their accessories the most. I bought some socks with spiders and skeletons here. And they've got cool bracelets."

He rolls up the sleeve of his hoodie and displays a black leather bracelet with metal hooks.

"And I found two sweaters I like here. They must be in one of the piles you saw in my room. I don't feel like wearing them to school, at least not right now. People wouldn't think I was a boy if they knew I wear clothes from here."

I put on a surprised look. "Sorry, I forgot to mention it. I told the journalist everything. You know, the one who wrote the article about you in the paper. He was scandalized, because you compete with boys in a swimming championship, but you wear clothes from Cruella!"

"Oh, no!" Liam cries in fake despair. "No psychologist will ever believe I'm really a boy!"

We go on joking until Liam finds the cap he covets. It really is beautiful. It's made of red and white striped cloth that looks like denim and suede at the same time, with two white Xs on the front, like eyes. Liam tries it on and considers his reflection in the mirror, looking much too serious, which is his natural state, if I understand correctly. The cap looks good on him, with his complexion and dark hair, but the style doesn't exactly suit his personality. I tell him I like the cap, because when he takes it off, he has this wide smile. He must really love it, he seems so delighted. I don't want to spoil his fun.

On the way to the cash, I stop to admire a dark

blue crinoline dress with ruffles. Extravagant—and wonderful.

"Hey, look at this. It's perfect."

"You would never dare wear that, anywhere!"

"You wouldn't say that if you knew me last year."

"You're right, I didn't know you. So, what's changed?"

I think about his question. Have I really changed? I've been in high school for two weeks. Every morning, a game of push and pull keeps me from dressing the way I want, in hopes of looking as normal as possible. What has that gotten me? The chance to sit at a lunch table with a larger number of people? If the new friends I've made through Stephie really care about me, the way I dress shouldn't bother them.

"I started wanting to fit in with everyone else. I think that's what has changed. You know, try and be like them."

"I understand. That's what I do too. You tell yourself nothing bad can happen if you slip under the radar."

"There's that, and there's the fact that I don't have very many friends. I'm afraid to lose the ones I do have if I step out of line."

I think of Stephie, and how afraid she is to reveal, even accidentally, that she's trans. I wouldn't want it to be my fault if people found out about her.

"Well, whatever you decide to wear, it's not going to keep me from being your friend."

He smiles. Liam smiles so rarely that, when he does, it touches my heart twice as much.

14

A Few Fashion Tips Before I Go

I wake up with a powerful feeling of feeling good. As I wait for the two minutes before my alarm sounds, I think of all the things I'm thankful for. My thick blanket that stays cool and soft through the night and welcomes my cheeks in the morning. My little brother snoring in the next room. I'm not thankful for his snoring, but for him being close by. And Stephie who is still my friend in spite of everything, and Liam, who I never thought would be my friend. My YouTube channel with its 250 subscribers, can you imagine that? Almost as many as there are first-year students in my high school. And now that I have my camera, pretty soon I won't have to wake up so early for the papers.

Beep-beep-beep!

I put on my pajama bottoms and a sweatshirt, and get ready for work. Outside, the sky is thick with clouds and the wind is blowing. Not great for getting around on a bike.

As I start out, I think of yesterday evening. After Liam bought the cap of his dreams, we went to his house so I could pick up my things. I didn't stay long, since he had swim practice. He has two practices during the week, and a session at the gym on weekends and exercises to do at home every evening. I said that was a lot, and he compared his schedule to the time and energy I spend on my YouTube channel, including delivering the paper, since that's how I financed my camera.

"We're alike that way, you and I," he told me. "We're willing to do what it takes to reach our goals."

I think he must be right. When I realize I have that determination, I feel very happy, and ready to do anything to get where I want to be.

When my paper route is finished, I go home. Through the clouds, the sun is starting to rise next to the mast of the Olympic Stadium. I'm brimming with energy, and full of self-confidence. It's a great feeling. Everyone is sleeping except for Borki, who comes to greet me, walks me to my room, and sits down in front of my door.

I open my closet and peer inside, my hands on my

hips. I think of the clothes I have worn since school began. Mentally, I roll them into a ball and toss them in the garbage. Then I go looking for my favorite outfits that have ended up at the back of the closet, since I've not been wearing them. I try on different combinations until I come up with one I like best: a white T-shirt with spangles (like we were back in 2015!), a skirt with peach-colored flounces, and striped leggings in all the colors of the rainbow. I'll just add dark eye shadow for the right dramatic effect! And I happen to have some I bought in August and haven't used. A violet shade, to bring out my green eyes. I saw that on a YouTube tutorial.

Once my makeup is just right, I take a few selfies and choose my favorite one. I think of sending it to Eiríkur, the way I used to. It hurts, but instead, I send it to Stephie, who will appreciate it more than my ex.

I take a quick look at YouTube. I have received a lot of new comments, most of them positive, since I reactivated the function, and more people have subscribed to my channel. I'm itching to know whether Bettie Bobbie Barton saw my latest video. I have not been identified anywhere, so maybe not, though I like to think she did see it, and that it shut her mouth once and for all.

♥ ♥ ♥

I prepared myself mentally before setting out for school, but still, it's strange to see so many eyes turning and staring as I walk down the hallway. I keep my head high as I reach our locker. Stephie is there, emptying her backpack. She looks my way, and I get a thumbs-up of approval.

"Now aren't you pretty this morning!"

I smile and open the locker door wider to look in the mirror, and make sure my eye shadow survived the bus ride.

"I figured the school needs a little more style."

"I have to tell you, with those neutral outfits you've been wearing since the beginning of the year, I was starting to worry you'd fallen into an emo phase, or something like that."

Our first classes are on the same floor, so we walk together.

"Did you try out your new camera last night?" Stephie asks, full of curiosity.

"I ran tests to see how it works. It's not so complicated after all."

"Was it fun with Liam?" she inquires slyly.

"It was. We went to Cruella afterward."

"You went without me?"

"He asked me to go," I protest, but just for the fun of it. "I couldn't tell him no."

"I didn't think that store was his style. I wish I'd been there."

As we walk down the hall, I catch some of the students staring. Stephie pretends not to notice.

"So when's your first date?" she asks.

"Are you asking how much time you have to steal him away for yourself?" I tease her.

"Don't worry, he's all yours!"

She laughs, then heads off to her class. I go into the science lab. Through the noise and action in the hallway, I hear the word *YouTube* spoken by a girl who points a discreet finger in my direction as she gossips with someone, right in front of me. I try to keep from blushing, but it's no use.

I go into class. My usual spot at the back is free. As I cross the room, heads turn my way. A boy I don't know calls out in a mocking voice.

"Cute dress!"

I don't waste time. "It's a skirt, silly!"

He stares at me, mouth open. Clearly, he wasn't expecting me to answer. To tell the truth, neither was I. But today is different. I run my hand through my hair to make sure my look is just right. My hair is soft to the touch. Maybe self-confidence works as a conditioner. Some of the students who heard my answer watch me, curious about what's going to come next. I sit down and smile, and hold their gaze. I'm ready to show them what I'm made of.

The End

About the Author

SOPHIE LABELLE is an internationally renowned visual artist and author from the South Shore of Montreal, in French Canada. She is the transgender cartoonist behind *Assigned Male*, a webcomic about a group of queer and trans teenagers that has been running since 2014 and has touched millions of readers. She lives in Finland.